Philip José Farmer has written over thirty novels and over fifty novellas and short stories, and between this book's publication and your reading it he will doubtless have written several more. But it is not simply his remarkably prolific output for which he is regarded as one of the very greatest science-fiction authors: his wild imagination, his equally wild sense of humour, his technical knowledge and his beautifully dry, satirical style of writing have also contributed to his reputation. Three times the winner of the coveted Hugo Award, official biographer of Tarzan and Doc Savage, Greek historian, mythologian and zeppelin freak, he's as amazing as but no less credible than a character from one of his own novels.

ALSO BY PHILIP JOSÉ FARMER AVAILABLE IN QUARTET PAPERBACKS

The Wind Whales of Ishmael
Timestop!
The Gate of Time

DARE

PHILIP JOSÉ FARMER

QUARTET BOOKS LONDON

First published in Great Britain by Quartet Books Limited 1974
27 Goodge Street, London W1P 1FD

ISBN 0 704 31165 8

Printed in Great Britain by
Hunt Barnard Printing Ltd, Aylesbury, Bucks

DARE

PROLOGUE

Where did they go?

One hundred and eight men, women, and children do not disappear from Earth without a trace.

The 'lost' colony of Roanoke, Virginia, did. Virginia Dare, first white baby born in North America, was among those never seen again. She and her English fellows and some Croatan Indians went – somewhere. Between 1587 and 1591 A.D. they – travelled.

Charles Fort, chronicler of the better-off-forgotten and explainer of the unexplainable, knew the above. But he did not know several other things. It is too bad, for he would have been delighted. The theories, the ironies, the sarcasms, the paradoxes that would have flowed from his pen!

Too bad that the disappearance of the Genovese ship *Buonavita* was not brought to Fort's notice by some South American correspondent. On May 8, 1588, she was last seen sixty leagues off the Grand Canary Islands by the Spanish caravel *Tobosa.*

Sailing under the Portuguese flag, she carried forty Irish and three Italian monks. They were bound for Brazil, where they hoped to convert the heathen. Neither Christian nor pagan saw them again.

Here.

In itself, the disappearance is not so noteworthy. Ships have long had a habit of dropping from the surface of evident things. The *Buonavita* is mentioned in various church histories and in a recent Brazilian history because the abbot of the monks was one Marco Sozzini, or, as he is most often called, Marcus Socinus. He was the nephew of the heretic Faustus Socinus, and a courier had been dispatched to Brazil with orders for Marcus to come to Rome, where he would face some questions.

That courier would not have been able to deliver his message even if he had known where Socinus was.

Another event at the same time would have made Fort sing with joy if it had been brought to his notice.

A book published in 1886 and now long out of print contains a translation of sections of Ibn Khulail's *History of the Turks*. By a Fortean coincidence, the translator was a Methodist minister, the Reverend Carl Fort. Taking the same interest in the unorthodox as his literary grandson, he records the Arab historian's description of the vanishing overnight of a large caravan.

In 1588 ninety Circassian beauties, destined for the harems of Moslem lords, and forty guards of various nationalities passed from man's sight. Their horses were found hobbled for the night. Their tents were still set up. Meals had grown cold waiting to be eaten.

The only sign of disorder was a bloody scimitar lying on the ground. Stuck in the blood were a dozen long, thick, and reddish hairs that the experts said were those of no known animal. Some people thought they might be from a bear, for the footprint of a tremendous ursine creature was found on the campsite.

Where, asked Ibn Khulail, did all those people go? Had a djinn flown away with them to some flame-guarded castle? Were those his hairs sticking to the blade?

History has no more answer for him than it has for those curious about Roanoke and the *Buonavita*.

Another item for Fort. The now defunct Aiguillette Press of Paris printed the essays of an eighteenth-century Chinese sage, Ho Ki. He remarks casually in his *Frost Thoughts* that the village of Hung Choo decided one night to go for a long walk and never came back.

That is all he says, except that the year they left was 1592 A.D.

From 1592 to 2092 is five hundred years, not such a long time in Earth's life. But from Earth to Dare is a long way, even as light flies. Dare is the second planet of a star classified as Tau Ceti by the moderns.

English is spoken there, Latin, and horstel.

An old map, drawn by Ananias Dare, father of Virginia, shows the continent on which the abducted Terrans were landed. Avalon they named it. The outlines, hastily inked as the planet grew larger and larger in the viewport, indicate a roughly four-lobed shape sprawling in the centre of a globe of water.

A cross marks the location of the first human settlement, originally titled New Roanoke. Later it was named Farfrom because the little Virginia Dare remarked that it was 'far from where I was born, Papa.'

Also on Dare's original cartograph are legends indicating where creatures strange to Earth but named after those that resembled Terrestrial beings, actual or mythical, were to be found.

'Here be unicorns . . . Here be man-eating werewolves.'

Many places, of course, are marked, simply, 'Horsetails.'

Jack Cage walked down the ancient highway. His high-crowned broad-brimmed hat kept off the hot, late-spring sun. Under its shadow his brown eyes searched the forests on both sides of the road. His left hand held a totumwood longbow. His quiver was full. A leather scabbard held a scimitar on his left; from the right of his broad belt hung a bag. It contained a round glass bomb filled with black gunpowder. A very short fuse jutted from its thick neck.

Beside the bag was a scabbard that sheathed a knife of red copperwood.

If the 'dragon' charged down the highway or burst out of the forest, Jack was ready for it. First, he would let fly an arrow at one of its huge eyes. Elsewhere would be useless. Flint tips wouldn't go through two inches of hard hide.

He had heard their bellies were soft, but he couldn't depend on that. Rumour could kill a cat, so the proverb went. He wasn't a cat – whatever a cat was – but he could be killed just as dead.

As if reading his thought, Samson, the giant yellow canine of the breed known as 'lion,' rumbled in his throat. He halted ten feet ahead of his master. Poised stiff-legged at right angles to Jack, he faced the trees to the left of the highway.

Jack drew an arrow from his quiver and fitted the notch to the string. He reviewed his plan. Shoot at the eye. Hit or miss, he would drop the bow. Snatch out the bomb. Touch off the fuse with a lucifer. Throw it at the monster's chest with the hope he'd timed the cast so the bomb would explode and crush its chest and drive the glass splinters into its throat.

Then, without waiting to see the effect of the powder, he'd turn and run, drawing his scimitar at the same time. Having gained a tree on the opposite side of the road, he'd stop to defend himself. He could dodge behind the large bole and slash out with the sword, circling around the trunk away from the large and presumably clumsy beast.

Meanwhile, Samson would harass the thing on its flanks.

He placed himself behind Samson. There was a slight break in the greenery. At the moment he glanced through it, something bright flashed. Unconsciously, he sighed with relief. He didn't know who was behind the glittering object, but he was fairly sure it wasn't a dragon. It should be a man or horstel.

As the arrow would be useless in the entangling bushes and vines, he put it back in the quiver. The bow he hung on a bonehook on his backstrap. He slid the scimitar from its sheath.

'Quiet, Samson,' he said in a low voice. 'Lead.'

The yellow dog padded ahead into a barely discernible path. Samson's nose bobbed up and down on the scent like a cork on a wave. He sniffed at the earth. Somebody had left tracks, for instead of taking a straight path, the 'lion' followed a serpentine track through the green labyrinth.

After about thirty yards of slow and cautious approach, they came to a little glade.

Samson stopped. The growl buried in his massive throat spoke through bristling hairs and rigid muscles.

Jack looked past him. He, too, froze. But it was with horror.

His cousin, Ed Wang, was crouched by the body of a satyr. It lay on its side, its back to Jack. Blood spread from the base of the spine. The shaggy hair that enclosed the loins was soaked with red.

Ed had a copperwood knife with which he was cutting away the skin around the tailbone. He stuck the knife into the ground and then ripped away the circle of tissue and the long 'horsetail' that grew from it. Rising, he held the bloody trophy in the sunlight, examining it.

'Bobbing?' asked Jack, the look on his cousin's face making him shudder. His voice sounded hoarse and phlegm-clotted.

Ed whirled, dropping the bob, and snatched up the knife. His mouth hung open. His black eyes were wide.

When he saw the intruder was Jack, he came out of the knife-fighter's crouch. Some of his colour returned, but he still held the blade ready in his fist.

'Holy Dyonis!' he croaked. 'For a second I thought you were a horstel.'

Jack nudged Samson with his knee. The dog padded out into the glade. Though he knew Ed, his stance threatened a swift bound at Ed's throat if he made an unwise move.

Jack lowered the scimitar, but he did not sheathe it. 'What if I had been a horstel?' he asked.

'Then I'd have had to kill you, too.'

Ed watched closely to see his cousin's reaction. Jack kept his face unreadable. Ed shrugged and turned away, slowly, and with one eye on Samson. He stooped and wiped his blade on the satyr's thick yellow hair.

'This is my first kill,' he said in a strained voice, 'but it's not my last.'

'Oh?' said Jack, and he managed with that one syllable to convey a mixture of disgust, fear, and the first intimations of just what this scene implied.

'Yes, oh!' mock-snarled Ed. His voice rose. 'I said it wasn't my last!'

He glared and stood up.

Jack knew that Ed was close to hysteria. He had seen his cousin in action in tavern brawls. His wild blows had endangered his friends as much as his enemies.

He said, 'Calm down, Ed. Do I look like a horstel?'

He stepped forward to look at the corpse's face. 'Who is it?'

'Wuv.'

'Wuv?'

'Yes, Wuv. One of the Wiyr living on your father's farm. I trailed him until I was sure he was alone. Then I got him into this glade on the pretext I wanted to show him a mandrake's nest. There wasn't any, of course, but while he was walking ahead of me, I stabbed him in the back.

'It was easy. He didn't even cry out. And after all that dung I'd heard about it being impossible to catch a horstel off guard! It was easy, I tell you! Easy!'

'For God's sake, Ed! Why? Why? What'd he do to you?'

Ed cursed. He stepped up to Jack, his copperwood blade flashing red as he stabbed upward.

Samson's deep chest rumbled, and he crouched. His master, taken unawares, brought up the scimitar for a swing to cut off his attacker's arm.

But Ed had stopped. As if he'd not seen the effect of his actions, he began talking. Jack lowered his sword, for it was evident that his cousin hadn't meant to attack, but had knifed the air to emphasise what he was saying.

'What reason should I need other than that he's a horstel? And I'm a human? Listen, Jack. You know Polly O'Brien, don't you?'

Jack blinked at what seemed a sudden change of subject, but he nodded. He remembered her very well. She lived in the town of Slashlark. She and her mother, the widow of a chemist, had recently moved from the capital city of St. Dyonis to the frontier town. There her mother had set up a shop and sold drugs, wine, ointments, and, so it was said, love-philters.

The first time he saw Polly, Jack had been impressed. She was slim, and her face was wonderfully heart-shaped, her eyes were large and an innocent-wanton grey, if you would admit such a description possible.

Jack, though he'd been going so long with Bess Merrimoth that he was ready to ask her parents if they could bundle, would have courted Polly, too. Even at the risk of getting his folks and Bess's mad at him. He had held back only because Ed Wang had announced at the Red Horn Tavern that he was squiring Polly O'Brien. As his friend, Jack could not decently cut in on him. Regretfully, he'd decided to leave her alone.

'Sure, I know her,' he replied. 'You were very sweet on her.'

Ed said loudly, 'Jack, she's taken *sanctuary!* She's gone cadmus!'

'Wait a minute! What's been going on? I've been up in the mountains for five days.'

'Holy Virginia, Jack! All hell's broken loose. Polly's mother was turned in for selling horstel drugs, and she was put in prison. Polly's wasn't accused, at first, that is, but when the sheriff came after her mother, she ran away. Nobody could find her, and then old Winnie Archard – you know her, Jack, she's got nothing to do but watch the road into Slashlark – saw Polly meet a satyr on the edge of town. She went away with him, and since she hasn't been seen again, it's easy to figure she went cadmus.'

He paused for breath and scowled.

'So?' said Jack with a coolness he didn't feel.

'So the next day the sheriff is told to arrest Polly. What a laugh! Did you ever hear of anybody being arrested once he'd gone underground with the horstels?'

'No.'

'You're damn right you didn't. I don't know what happens after they go down the cadmus. Whether the horstels eat them, as some say, or whether they're smuggled to Socinia, as others say. But I do know one thing. That is that Polly O'Brien isn't going to get away from me!'

'You're in love with Polly, aren't you, Ed?'

'No!'

Ed looked up at his tall relative; then he flushed and lowered his eyes.

'All right. Yes, I *was*. But no more. I hate her, Jack. I hate her for a witch. I hate her for lying with a satyr.

'Don't look so damned doubtful, Jack. I mean that. She was buying drugs from the horstels, and she was meeting this Wuv secretly to get them. She was making love to him. Can you picture that, Jack? A wild, naked, hairy-loined beast. She was meeting him, and I – I . . . I could throw up when I think of her!'

'Who laid the charges against Mrs O'Brien?'

'I don't know. Somebody sent letters to the bishop and the sheriff. The identity is always kept secret, you know.'

Jack rubbed the side of his nose and mouth thoughtfully and said, 'Wasn't Nate Reilly's chemistry shop losing business because he couldn't compete with Polly's mother?'

Ed smiled faintly. 'You're smart. Yes, he was. And everybody's more or less guessed who informed. Mainly because Nate's wife has the biggest mouth in Slashlark, which is saying something.

'But what about it? If Mrs O'Brien was trafficking in those devil-begotten drugs, she deserved to get turned in, whatever Reilly's motive.'

'What's happened to Mrs O'Brien?'

'She was sentenced to hard labour for life at the gold mines in Ananias Mountains.'

Jack's thick eyebrows rose. 'Sort of a quick trial, wasn't it?'

'No! She confessed within six hours of being arrested, and she was sent away two days later.'

'Six hours on the rack would make anybody confess. What if the local Binder of the Contract hears of that?'

'You sound like you're defending her. You know that when

anybody is as clearly guilty as she was, a little torture just helps speed justice. And the horstels aren't going to find out about the machines in the prison basement. And what if they do? So we've broken our contract with them? So what?'

'So you think Polly's hiding in the cadmi on my father's farm?'

'Damn right I do. And I was going to corner Wuv and force him to tell me about her, but when I was alone with him, I became so angry I couldn't hold myself back. And – '

He gestured toward the corpse.

Jack, following the motion, suddenly pointed the scimitar and cried, 'What's that?'

Wang bent down and lifted the head of the corpse by its long hair. The jaw sagged and pulled the flesh down so the knife cuts on each cheek stretched.

'See those letters? HK? You're going to see a lot of those from now on. Someday you'll see them on the cheeks of every horstel in Dyonis. Yes, and if we can get co-operation from the other nations, all over Avalon. Every horstel marked, and every horstel dead!'

Jack Cage said slowly, 'I've heard some talk in the taverns about a secret society dedicated to killing horstels. But I didn't believe it. In the first place, it couldn't be much of a secret if all the drunks knew about it. In the second place, I just thought it was the kind of talk you're always hearing when men talk about The Problem. Always talk. Never action.'

'By all that's human and holy, you're going to see action now!'

Ed removed the bag hanging by a rope from his shoulder. 'Come on. Help me bury this carcass.'

He pulled from the bag a short-handled shovel with a scoop made of the new Hardglass. The sight of it horrified Jack almost as much as the body had. Its presence showed such cold-blooded planning.

Wang started cutting out divots of the short-bladed crop-grass and placing them to one side. While he was doing that he talked, and he did not stop all the time he was digging the shallow grave.

'You're not a member of the society yet, but you're in this just as much as I am. I'm glad it was you and not some other human that found me. Some of those lickspittle yellow-livered horstel-lovers would run screaming to the sheriff instead of shaking my hand.

'Of course, if they did, they wouldn't last long. It isn't only horstels that can get their cheeks marked. Human flesh, traitor flesh, will cut just as easily. You understand?'

Numbly, Jack shook his head. He had to declare himself either for Ed, who identified himself with the human race, or against him. And he could not do the latter. He was sickened by what had happened; he wished that Samson had not caught the scent of death and that he'd not seen the flash of the knife in the break. He would have liked to turn and run away and try to forget all about this; deny it, if possible, tell himself it had never happened, or if it had, that he had nothing to do with it. But he couldn't do that. And now . . .

'Here, grab his leg,' Ed said. 'I'll take the other, and we'll drag him to the grave.'

Jack put the scimitar in its scabbard. Together, he and Ed pulled the body across the glade, its limp arms trailing behind like idle oars beside a drifting boat. Blood left a red wake on the crushed grass.

'We'll have to clip off that grass and throw it in the grave, too,' Ed spoke. He was panting.

Cage nodded. He had wondered why Ed, a short but very strong man, had wanted him to help haul the corpse the mere thirty feet to the hole. Now he saw. His helping to bury the victim would be his share in the guilt.

The worst of it was that he couldn't refuse to join. Not that he was forced to because he was afraid, he hastened to assure himself. He had no fear of Ed or of the vaster, if more shadowy figure behind him, the HK Society. It was just that horstels weren't human. They didn't have souls, even if they did, hair distribution apart, look like men.

It wasn't murder to kill one, not murder in a real sense; legally, it was. But no human thought of it as actual murder. Killing a dog wasn't murder. Why should slaying one of the Wiyr be?

There were a number of reasons why the courts considered it so. The strongest was that they were compelled to do so. The Dyonisan government had a contract that set up judicial procedure for just such man-horstel dealings. But no human should feel a sense of guilt, of having offended his God because of the dead.

Why, then, this twisting inside himself?

Automatically, he said, 'Do you think the grave is deep

enought? Wild dogs or werewolves could dig him up easily.'

'That's using your head, Jack. For a moment I thought . . . Well, never mind. Sure, the dogs can get at him. But they won't. Watch.'

He dipped into his bag and brought out a small bottle of clear fluid.

'Nodor. It'll cover up any smell for twenty-four hours. By then the sextons will have finished him. Nothing but bones left.'

He sprinkled the bottle's contents over the corpse. The fluid spread in a thin film over the body until it disappeared.

Ed walked around the glade, letting fall a drop or two wherever he saw blood or crushed grass. Satisfied he'd fairly well deodorized the place, he picked up the long blond bob from the ground, threw a couple of drops on it, and stuffed it into his bag.

He said, casually, 'Do you want to cover up the body?'

Jack gritted his teeth and stood motionless for a minute. Refusal trembled on his tongue. He wanted to yell out, 'Killer! Killer!' and walk away. But reason held him silent. Either he went along with Ed now, hoping for a break later on, or – and his mind did not refuse the picture as the next plausible step, though his stomach did – he could kill Ed and tumble his body into the hole.

Monstrous as it seemed, that would be the only way to prevent the entanglements sure to come. He had to join the HK, or else he had to die.

Sighing, he began scooping dirt on the body. 'Hey, Jack, look at that!'

Jack looked past Ed's extended finger and saw a sexton crouching beneath a fallen leaf. It was no longer than the knucklebone of his thumb, and its long thin nose quivered ceaselessly. Then it was gone, swifter than his eye could follow.

'How much do you want to bet that by tonight he and his thousand brothers will have all the meat off the satyr's bones?'

'Yes,' replied Jack sourly. 'And when those scavengers are through, the dirt over the bones will sink down and leave a depression. If it's noticed and he's dug up by the Wiyr, they'll know he's been murdered. You'd have been smarter if you'd just left the body above ground. That way, they'd have no way of telling from the bones what had happened to him. His death would be considered accidental, or at least from causes unknown. This way, they know it's murder.'

'You should have planned this, Jack,' said Ed. 'You're smart. I can see you're going to be a big asset to the society.'

Jack grunted and then said, 'On second thought, that half-severed spine would give it away. Maybe it's better he's buried.'

'See what I mean? You'd have sense enough not to touch his backbone when you stabbed him. I can tell you're going to make a great killer, Jack.'

Jack didn't know whether to laugh or weep.

Ed watched his tall cousin as he smoothed out the grave to make it level with the surrounding ground. He spoke harshly, as if he were trying to get something out before he changed his mind and kept it in.

'Jack, you want to know something? I like you, but personal feelings don't enter. When I first saw you, I thought I might have to kill you, too, in order to shut you up. But you're all right. You're all human.'

'I'm human,' answered Jack. He kept on working. While Ed clipped off the bloodstained grass ends, Jack carefully replaced the divots over the naked earth. That done, he rose to examine his work.

He wasn't satisfied. If the forest-wise Wiyr got close, they'd detect the artificiality of the replaced cropgrass. The only chance to escape notice would be if the hunters overlooked the glade or if they went over it carelessly. Knowing the aborigines' thoroughness, he did not feel easy.

He said, 'Ed, is this the first murder for you? Or for other HK members?'

'It's not murder! It's war! Remember that! Yes, it's the first for me. But not for others. We've secretly killed two other horstels here in Slashlark County. One was a siren.'

'Have any HK members disappeared mysteriously?'

Ed jerked as if struck. 'What makes you ask that?'

'The horstels are smart. You think for a minute they won't figure out what's going on? And play the game themselves?'

Ed Wang swallowed. 'They wouldn't do that! They have a contract with our government. If they caught us, they're bound by their word to leave us to the human courts.'

'How many government officials are HK members?'

'Know what, Jack? There is such a thing as being too smart.'

'Not really. What I'm getting at, though, is that the Wiyr are realists. They know that, legally, a human killer of a horstel is subject to the death penalty. They also know that, actually, it's almost impossible to convict a man in our courts on such a charge.

'It's true that a horstel's word is his bond. But they have a clause that says that if the other party proves to be of bad faith, the contract is automatically broken.'

'Yes, but they have to give the other party notice.'

'True. But tension is getting high. One of these days, there's going to be a bad break. The horstels know that. Maybe they're going to organise their own HK – the Human Killers.'

'You're crazy! They wouldn't do anything like that. Besides, no HK men are missing.'

Jack decided he was getting noplace. He said, 'There's a brook close by. We'd better wash. And then put on some of that Nodor ourselves. You know what a sensitive nose a horstel has.'

'Like an animal's. They're beasts of the field, Jack.'

After they'd washed themselves and smoothed out the footprints they'd made in the mud banks, they decided to separate.

'I'll give you the word when we have our next meeting,' promised Ed. 'Say, what about bringing your sword to it? Outside of Lord How's, it's the only iron weapon in the county. It'd make a wonderful symbol of our organisation, a sort of rallying point.'

'It's my father's. I took it without his permission when I went dragon hunting. What he'll say when I get back, I don't know. But I'll bet he locks it up where I can't get it again.'

Ed shrugged, smiled an unreadable smile, and said goodbye.

Jack watched him go. Then, shaking his head like a man trying to wake himself up, he walked away.

Walt Cage strode from the barn and through the yard. His boots stomped into the wet ground and squished as he pulled them out. The gagglers in his path fled, giving vent to a nerve-scraping cry. Away from his dangerous feet, they stopped to look with their big double-lidded blue eyes. They teetered on two long thin legs and flapped their rudimentary wings – membranes stretched on long fingerbones – and cocked their smear-nosed heads. The nursers gave a series of thin barks that called their chicks to feed from two swollen mammaries hanging between their legs. The egg-hens jealously bit at the nursers with tiny sharp teeth and then fled as the big cocks chased them back to their nests. Now and then, the males lunged at each other and nipped, but they didn't mean it. Their stud-fury had been watered with centuries of domestication.

All shared a powerful odor that was a cross between that of an open garbage can in the hot sun and that of a wet dog. It insulted and injured even the most tolerant nose. Serene, they dwelt in the midst of it and minded not at all.

Walt Cage snarled 'Aggh!' and spat at them. Then he felt mildly ashamed of himself. After all, the dumb brutes could not help their stench. And their meat and eggs did taste delicious and were quite profitable.

He was headed for the front porch of his house when he remembered the mud on his boots. Kate would kill him if he tracked dirt once again into the front room. He steered toward his office. Bill Kamel, his overseer, would probably be waiting there, anyway.

Bill was sitting in his boss's chair, smoking a pipe and resting his muddy boots on Walt's desktop. When the owner burst through the door, Bill jumped up so fast the chair fell back and on to the floor.

'Go ahead,' Walt barked. 'Don't mind me.'

When Kamel made an irresolute move to pick up the chair and sit down, Walt brushed by him and seated himself, hard. He groaned, 'What a day! I couldn't get anything done. I hate shearing unicorns, anyway. And those horstels! Always stopping to sample that new batch of wine.'

Bill coughed self-consciously and blew smoke to one side.

'Don't worry about my smelling your breath,' Walt growled. 'I had a glass or two myself.'

Bill blushed. Walt leaned forward and picked up a pencil. 'All right. Let's have it.'

Bill closed his eyes and began the report. 'All plows are now fitted with new copperwood blades. Our agent in Slashlark says he can get one of those Hardglass blades for experimental purposes. Cheap. It should be here in about a week since it's coming by boat. They're supposed to keep their edge twice as long as the wooden. I told him you said you'd replace all our blades with them if the glass worked out like it was supposed to . . . right? And he said he'd knock off ten percent of the price if we'd recommend the blades to our neighbours.

'The Herder of the Unicorns says the thirty foals he started working with are narrowed down to five. They might be good plowers, and they might not. You know how nervous and unreliable those beasts are.'

'Of course, I know!' said Walt Cage impatiently. 'You think I've been farming for twenty years for nothing? Dyonis, how I hate spring plowing, and how I hate unicorns! Oh, if we only had an animal that could pull a plow without trying to run away every time a lark flies over and throws its shadow!'

'The Counter of the Bees reports there's a lot of noise in the hives. He estimates we've about fifteen thousand bees. They ought to be coming out by next week. The winterhoney crop will be smaller this year because there's been more young to feed.'

'That means less money for all. Isn't anything going right?' demanded Walt.

'Well, next spring there'll be more honey because there've been more young this winter.'

'Use your head, Bill. Those young'll produce more young and eat up all the winterhoney. Don't tell me how big the crop's going to be!'

'That isn't what the Counter says. He says that every third year the queens eat up the surplus brats so the honey crop'll be larger. Next year's the third.'

'Good!' broke out Walt. 'I'm glad something's going to go right around here. But the taxes next year are going up, and I'll have a hard time paying a tax on a larger crop. Last year's hurt me, as it was.'

Bill looked blankly at him and continued. 'The Catcher of the Larks says the egg collection will be about the same as last year's, about ten thousand. That is, unless the werewolves and the maskers increase, in which case we'll be lucky to get half that.'

'I knew it,' groaned Cage. 'I knew it, and I was depending on the egg profits to pay for the new plow blades. And buy a new carriage.'

'We don't know the collection won't be up to last year's,' Bill said.

'Listen, those satyrs sleep with Old Mother Nature. They know her as a man knows his wife. Better,' added Walt, as certain doubts about his Kate came to his mind.

'If the Catcher thinks the werewolves'll increase, they will. And that means I'll have to hire some guards from Slashlark and maybe pay for a big hunt.'

Kamel's brows rose, and he puffed angrily as he restrained himself from showing the boss how he was contradicting himself about the horstels' reliability.

Cage's eyes narrowed as he pulled at the hairs of his thick black beard as if they were ripe thoughts to be plucked.

'Lord How has a stake in keeping the werewolves down. Maybe he could foot the bill. If I could only drop a few words about it to him and let him mull over it until he thinks it's his own idea, he might organize one. If I didn't have to pay for food for the hunters and dogs . . . '

He licked his lips, smiled, and rubbed his big hands. 'Well, we shall see. Go on.'

'The Keeper of the Orchard says the totum crop should be bigger than ever. Last year we collected sixty thousand balls. This year the Keeper estimates seventy thousand. Providing the slashlarks don't increase.'

'What next? Every time you tell me something, I'm a rich man in one breath and a poor in the next. Well, don't just sit there and smoke. Tell me, what does the Catcher of the Larks say?'

Bill shrugged. 'He says there should be an increase by at least a third.'

'More expense!'

'Not necessarily. The Blind King remarked to me last night that he can get help from a nomadic group of his people, and it won't cost anything except their food and wine. And he'll split the bill with you.'

Bill paused and wondered if he should give Walt the bad news he'd been saving. He wasn't given a chance, for the boss said, 'Did you check up on the Keeper of the Orchard's tally?'

'No, I didn't think it was necessary. The Wiyr don't lie.'

His face red, Walt roared, 'Of course not! Not as long as they know we'll always check up on them.'

Kamel's cheeks reflected the heat in Cage's, and he opened his mouth to reply. Then he shrugged and closed his lips.

Walt spoke in a softer tone, 'Bill, you're too easygoing. Trusting the horstels can get you in trouble.'

Bill focused his eyes on a spot above Cage's balding head and meditatively blew smoke.

'For heaven's sake, Bill, quit shrugging every time I say something. You trying to make me mad?'

'No. I don't have to try.'

'All right. So I asked for that. Maybe I do fly off the handle now and then. But I'm not the only one. The very air seems to quiver like a tightrope. Enough of that. What're you doing about setting a night watch for that dragon?'

'The horstels say the dragon'll take a few unicorns and then won't be back until next year. Nobody'll get hurt as long as it's not attacked. Just leave it alone.'

Cage brought his fist down hard on the desktop. 'Oh, so I'm to sit on my fat butt and watch that monster run off with my stock! You put Job and Al to building a trap.'

Bill said, 'What about Jack? Maybe he's killed it.'

'Jack's a fool!' roared Walt. 'I told him to wait until a hunting party was organised. After the unicorn shearing and the spring plowing, of course. I can't spare a man or horstel now.

'But that accursed fool, that brainless romantic idiot son of mine has to go gallivanting after something that could crush him with a flick of its tail. Why, that hulking overgrown good-for-nothing is senseless enough to attack that thing all by himself! And get his head bitten off! He will bring grief to his mother and make an old man of his father!'

Tears ran down his cheeks and sopped his beard. Choking, half-blinded, he rose and lurched from the office. Kamel was left staring embarrassedly at his pipe and wondering when he could tell him the really bad news.

In the washroom, Walt Cage poured out a pitcher of freshly drawn well water into a bowl and slapped water on his face. The tears quit flowing; his shoulders ceased shaking. Taking off his sleeveless jacket, he cleaned his arms and torso thoroughly. The mirror reflected the puffy and bloodshot eyes, but he could blame that on the little hairs floating around in the shearing shed. Bill was a good fellow and wouldn't say a word about his breaking down. Nobody else need know. It would never do for his family to find out, for then they might have less respect for him. They were getting hard enough to handle as it was. A man never cried; tears were for women...

He combed his beard and thanked God he hadn't succumbed to the new foppery and shaved off his whiskers. He didn't look like a woman or a barefaced satyr. It was a fashion that indicated the insidious horstel influence.

As he was putting on a clean flannel vest, sleeveless and tied loosely across the front so his hairy chest and belly stuck out brown and black and gray, he heard the dinner drum. He took off his dirty boots and put on clean slippers. Then he strode into the dining room and there paused to look around.

His children were standing behind their chairs, waiting until he seated their mother at the foot of the table before they sat down. His quick green eyes took in his sons Walt, Alec, Hal, Boris, and Jim, and his daughters Ginny, Betty, Mary, and Magdalene. Two chairs were empty.

Kate, anticipating his question, said, 'I sent Tony down the road to look for Jack.'

Walt grunted and seated Kate. He noticed that the rash that had broken out on her several days ago was getting worse. If it continued to ridge and redden her usually cream-smooth skin, he would take her into Slashlark and let Dr Chander look at her. As soon as the shearing was done, that was.

When he had seated himself at the head of the table, Lunk Croatan, the house servant, lurched from the kitchen. He almost tipped the platter of steaming unicorn 'mutton' onto his master's lap.

Walt sniffed and said, 'Been sampling the totum wine again, eh, Lunk? Hanging around with the satyrs?'

'Why not?' replied Lunk in a rough voice. 'They're getting ready for a big celebration. The Blind King's just learned his son and daughter are coming back tonight from the mountains. You know what that means. Lots of music, singing, barbecued unicorn and roasted dog, wine, beer, storytelling, and dancing.

'And,' he concluded maliciously, 'no shearing. Not for three days, anyway.'

Walt stopped carving the mutton. 'They can't do that! They've a contract to help shear. Why, three days' delay will mean we'll lose half our wool. By the end of this week, the beasts'll start shedding. Then what?'

Swaying, Lunk said, 'Nothing to worry about. They'll call in the forest dwellers to help. And everything'll be finished on schedule. So why get hysterical? We'll all have a good time and then work hard to catch up.'

'Shut up!' growled Cage.

'I'll speak when I want to,' Lunk said with a dignity that was lessened somewhat by the back-and-forth movement of his body. 'I'm no longer an indentured servant, I'll remind you. I've worked myself out of debt, and I may leave any time I want to. So what do you think of that?'

He walked slowly from the room.

Walt jumped up so fast his chair fell back and struck the floor. 'What's the world coming to? There's no respect any longer for those who deserve it. Servants . . . the younger generation . . . '

He struggled for words. 'No beards . . . all the young men smooth-shaven and letting their hair grow long . . . the women at court wearing low-cut bodices, exposing their breasts as if they're sirens. Even some of the officials' wives at Slashlark are imitating the custom . . . none of my daughters, thank God, would have the daring and indecency to wear such gowns!'

He glared about the table. His girls glanced at each other from under downcast lids. They'd never be able to wear those new costumes to the Military Ball now! Not unless they added much more lace to the open deep V's. Thank goodness the dressmaker hadn't brought them out to the farm yet!

Their father waved his knife and threw juice on Boris' new vest and shouted, 'It's horstel influence, that's what it is! By God, if the human race had iron to make guns, we'd wipe out the godless, savage, naked, immoral, indecent, lazy, drunken, arrogant, contract-making race! Look at the effect they've had on Jack. He's always been too friendly with them. He's not only learned child-horstel, but he knows much adult-talk. He's been seduced by their devil-inspired whisperings to give up working the farm – my farm! – the farm of his grandfather, may he rest in peace!

'Why do you think he's risking his life by hunting that dragon? To get the bounty for the head so he can go to Far-from and study under Roodman, a man who's been investigated for heresy and demon-dealings . . .

'Why, why, even if he does bring back the dragon's head, though probably his body is torn to pieces and lying scattered in some lost thicket . . . '

Kate cried, 'Walt!' and Ginny and Magdalene gave little cries.

'Why can't he use the bounty – if he gets it – as a dowry for Elizabeth Merrimoth's hand? Unite his farm and fortune and hers? She's the prettiest girl in the county, and her father is, next to Lord How, the richest man. Let him marry her and raise children for the greater glory of State, Church, and God – not to mention the delight it would bring to my heart.'

Lunk Croatan came back from the kitchen. He was carrying a huge bowl of egg pudding.

When Walt shouted his last statement, Lunk closed his eyes, shuddered, and said loudly, 'Dear Lord, preserve us from such satanic pride!' He stepped forward. His bare toe caught on the edge of a tailbear rug, and he pitched forward. The bowl up-ended over Walt's balding head; the hot thick pudding cascaded over his face, creamed his beard, and poured down his clean vest.

Yelling with pain, surprise, and fury, he jumped up. At that moment there was a shriek just outside the dining-room window. A second later, little Tony ran into the room.

He was shouting, 'Jack's coming! He's coming! And we're rich! We're rich!'

Jack Cage heard the siren singing.

She was far off, and she was close. She was the shadow of a voice demanding that the substance of the owner be found.

He left the highway and disappeared into the thick greenery. Samson's yellow bulk preceded him. The twang of a lyre vibrated through the winding green aisles. After he'd twisted and turned through narrow bole-lined avenues, he halted to reconnoiter. The forest broke away in a green rush from a little glade that was a cup of molten sunlight. In its center was a large granite boulder, twice as tall as a man. The upper part had been carved into a chair.

The siren sat in the chair, and she sang. While her lovely and strange song rose, she combed her long red-gold hair with the dried shell of a lake cilia. Beneath her, squatting at the base of the boulder and plucking the lyre strings, was a satyr, a male horstel.

She was looking through a break in the glade – a tree-lined boulevard that sloped down the mountainside and gave a view of much of the country north of Slashlark. Jack could see his father's farm. It was so far away it seemed as small as the palm of his hand, but he could make out the white coats and horns of the unicorns flashing in the sun as they bent their heads to the grass or raced across the meadows.

For a minute, he was distracted from the horstels by a wave of homesickness. The main house glittered redly as the sun bounced off the crystals that lodged in the copperwood logs.

It was a two-storey building, sturdily built and flat-roofed so men could walk on its top while withstanding sieges. A well was in the middle of the courtyard, and at each of the four roof corners was a catapult, a bomb-thrower.

Nearby was the barn. Beyond it was the checkered pattern of fields and orchards. On a meadow at the farm's far north end rose twelve gleaming white fangs of ivory, teeth from the earth, the cadmi.

The highway that ran by the farm could be traced in most of its wanderings until it reached the county seat of Slashlark. The town itself was hidden by a rise of heavily wooded hills.

He was recalled to his immediate surroundings when the siren stood up to launch her final greetings to the country to which she and her male companion were returning after three years of 'rites' in the remote mountains.

A notch in the trees outlined her against the light-blue sky. Jack sucked in his breath in sudden admiration. She was a splendid specimen – beautiful from a thousand years' breeding. Like all Wiyr, she wore nothing except a comb in her hair. At the moment, she was passing its teeth through the thick red-gold swarm. The left breast, following the arm's movements, tilted and dipped like the muzzle of some Euclidean animal feeding upon the air. And Jack's eyes fed upon its beauty.

A breeze lifted a tress and revealed a humanly shaped ear. She turned slightly and disclosed a quite unhuman distribution of hair. A thick, almost manelike growth sprouted from the base of her neck and grew in a spinal roach. From the tip of her backbone it fell in a cascade – the horsetail.

Her broad shoulders were as hairless as a woman's, as was the rest of her back except the vertebral column. Jack could not see her from the front, but he knew her loins were tufted. A horstel's pubic hair was long and thick enough to satisfy the humans' desire for genital covering; it hung like a loincloth halfway down the thighs.

The males were as shaggy between navel and midthigh as the mythic satyr from whom they derived their name. The females, however, had hips naked except for the pubic triangle, which was really a diamond, as the base of another three-cornered shape grew from it, sloped up the belly, and tapered off at the hair-ringed navel, which looked like an eye balanced on the apex of a shiny gold pyramid.

That was the Wiyr symbol for a female—omnicron speared by a delta.

Lost in admiration, Jack waited until the lyre *tmmmed* its final note and the siren's creamy contralto cast the end phrase down the green isle.

For a moment, there was silence. She stood poised like a bronze statue topped with gold; the satyr crouched over his instrument, eyes closed and brooding.

Jack stepped from behind a spearnut tree and clapped his hands. The explosion was like an unwarranted, even profane, intrusion upon the semireligious silence that had followed the music. Probably the two had sunk into one of their voluntary, half-mystic states.

Neither seemed startled or even surprised. Jack, maliciously, had hoped they would be. But their calm turning of eyes toward him and the grace of their bodies in following the eyes twinged him with annoyance and faint shame. Did they never appear awkward or embarrassed?

'Good afternoon, Wiyr,' he said.

The satyr stood up. His fingers ran over the lyre strings in simulation of an English voice. 'Good afternoon,' the strings spoke.

The female stuck the comb into her hair, poised like a diver on the rock, and jumped to the ground. Her bent knees took the shock easily; the impact bounced her large, conoid breasts in a movement that disconcerted Jack. Before the quivering had ceased, she had walked up to him. Her purple-blue irises contrasted pleasingly with the sinister cat-yellow of her brother's.

'How are you, Jack Cage?' she said in English. 'Don't you know me?'

Jack blinked down at her with a start of recognition. 'R'li! Little R'li! But you – holy Dyonis! – how you've changed! Grown!'

She ran a hand through her hair. 'Naturally. I was fourteen when I went into the mountains three years ago for the rites. Seventeen means I'm an adult. Is there anything surprising in that?'

'Yes . . . no . . . that is . . . you were built like a broom . . . that is . . . and now . . . ' Automatically, his hand described a curve.

She smiled and said, 'You needn't blush so. I know I have a beautiful body. However, I like compliments, and you may give me as many as you want to. Provided you're sincere about it.'

Jack felt his face warming. 'You . . . you misunderstand. I . . .' and he choked, helpless before the terrible candor of the horstel.

She must have felt sorry for him, for she tried to divert the talk away from them. 'Do you have a smoke on you?' asked R'li. 'We ran out a few days ago.'

'I've three. Just enough.'

He took a case out of his jacket pocket. It was made of expensive copper and had been given to him by Bess Merimoth. From it he shook out three rolls of coarse brown paper containing tobacco. Unconsciously, he offered the first to R'li because she was a female. His hand forgot to play the customary rude role of the human dealing with the horstel.

He did, however, stick a roll in his own lips before he offered her brother one. The satyr must have noticed the slight, for he smiled in a peculiar fashion.

When R'li bent over to light her roll on the lucifer Jack struck for her, she looked up. Her purple-blue eyes were as lovely as – he could not help thinking – Bess Merrimoth's. He'd never been able to see what his father meant by saying that gazing into their eyes was gazing into a beast's.

She drew smoke deep into her lungs, coughed, and blew clouds from her nostrils. 'A poison,' she said. 'But I like it. One of the gifts you humans brought from Terra was tobacco. I wonder how we got along without it?'

Was she being sarcastic? If so, she was so subtle about it that he couldn't be sure. 'That seems to be about the only vice you picked up from us,' he replied. 'It's the only gift you've taken. And that is something nonessential.'

She smiled. 'Oh, not the only gift. We eat dogs, you know.' She looked at Samson. He, as if sensing what she was talking about, edged closer to his master. Jack could not keep from showing his disgust.

'You needn't worry, big lion,' she called out to Samson. 'We never cook your breed. Just fat and stupid frydogs.'

She turned back to Jack.

'As to what we were talking about, you shouldn't feel that you Terrans came to us barehanded. We've learned much more from you than you think.'

Again she smiled. Jack felt foolish – as if the lessons administered by the human beings had been negative. Mrrn, her brother, spoke to her in rapid adult-talk. She answered the few syllables needed (translated into English, Jack suspected, the conversation would have taken much more time), and then said in the human tongue, 'He wants to stay here and work on a new song he's been thinking about. He'll play it tomorrow at our homecoming. I'll accompany you as far as my uncle's. That is, if you don't mind?'

He shrugged. 'Why should I?'

'I can think of half a dozen reasons. First and foremost, some human might see us and turn you in for fraternizing with a siren.'

'Walking on a public highway with one of you doesn't legally constitute fraternizing.'

They walked silently down the leafy corridor to the road. Samson walked a little ahead. Behind them, the notes charged from the lyre in a phalanx of fury. Where his sister's singing had been sweet and happy and tinged with a certain spriteliness, Mrrn's playing was Dionsiac, frenzied.

Jack would have liked to stay to hear it. Though he had, of course, never confessed it, he thought horstel music was wonderful. No reasonable excuse for lingering came to his mind, so he kept on going down the forest aisle. When they reached the road and turned the corner, the notes became faint. The towering trees and heavy foliage blanketed them.

The road curved around the gently sloping mountain – a fifty-foot broad highway at least a thousand years old. It was composed of some very thick gray stuff that must have been poured out in liquid form and then hardened, for it was not laid down in blocks but presented a continuous strip. Resembling stone, it felt slightly rubbery and gave the illusion of sinking a little beneath one's weight. Though the sun was hot, the road felt cool to the naked foot. Somehow, it passed heat through the upper side and stored it beneath, for during the winter the process was reversed. Then the surface radiated warmth, enough to keep the unshod foot from freezing even in the coldest weather. Snow and ice melted and ran off the subtly tilted slope.

It was one of the thousands that spider-webbed the continent of Avalon, a network whose ready transportation had helped humankind spread so rapidly across the land.

He was silent so long that R'li, probably seeking a hook on which to hang conversation, asked to see his scimitar. Surprised, he unsheathed it and handed it to her. Holding it by the hilt with one hand, she feather-touched the sharp edge with the fingers of the other.

'Iron,' she said. 'That is a terrible word for a terrible thing. I wonder what kind of world we'd have if there were much of it left. Not so good, I think.'

Jack watched her handle the metal. One of the tales he'd heard in his childhood about horstels had just been proved false. They could touch iron. Their fingers didn't wither, their arms didn't become paralyzed, and they didn't scream with agony.

She pointed to the inscription on the hilt. 'That means what?'

'I don't really know. It's said to be Erbic, one of the languages of Earth.'

He took the weapon back from her and turned the hilt to show her two inscriptions on the other side. 'One A.H.D. One of the year of Homo Dare. The year we came. Cut by Ananias Dare himself, so it's said. This sword was given by Kamel the Turk to Jack Cage the First, one of his sons-in-law, because the Turk had no sons to hand it on to.'

She said, 'Is it true that your scimitar is so sharp that it will cut a floating hair in half?'

'I don't know. I've never tried it.'

She plucked one of her long hairs out and let it drift down.

Swish!

Two red-gold threads fell to the ground.

'Do you know,' she said, 'you might have given that dragon something to think about, after all.'

His jaw fell, and he goggled while she ground the glowing butt of her smoke into dead ashes with her callused heel.

'How – how did you know I'd been trailing that dragon?'

'The dragon told me.'

'The dragon – *told* you?'

'Yes. You didn't miss her by much. She was with us for a while but left about five minutes before you showed up. She was getting tired of running. She's pregnant, and she's hungry, and she's exhausted. I advised her to go up the mountains to the rocky parts, where you wouldn't be able to find any tracks.'

'Well, now, isn't that nice!' His voice shook. 'And just how the hell would you know she knew I knew – I mean – she knew I was coming and she was going . . . I mean, how did you know where she was going? I suppose you spoke to her in dragon-talk?' he concluded sarcastically.

'Right.'

'What?'

He looked into her eyes for a sign she was pulling his leg. You never knew about Wiyr.

She returned his gaze with two cool purple-blue enigmas. There was a swift exchange, voiceless but intelligible. R'li put out her hand as if to place it on his arm and then stopped it midway as if suddenly remembering that human beings did not care to be touched by her people. Samson growled warningly and crouched facing her, yellow hair bristling.

They continued walking. She chattered blithely on as if nothing untoward had happened. To add to his annoyance, she used child-horstel. An adult used that tongue to another only in anger or contempt or to a loved one. She couldn't be in love with him.

She spoke of her happiness at coming home and seeing her friends and parents again and roaming the beloved fields and forest of Slashlark County. She smiled often; her eyes glowed with intense feeling; her hands flew as if she were batting the words out of the way in order to make room for more; her red mouth shaped itself into fascinating spouts as she spilled out the liquids of her speech.

A strange and unexpected thing happened to him as he watched the writhing mouth. His anger shifted to desire. He wanted to crush her to him, grab the red-gold cataract down her back, and bury that mouth beneath his. It was a swift and treacherous thought, and it surged through his blood stream, roared in his head, and almost overpowered him.

He turned his head away so she wouldn't see his face. His chest swelled until it seemed it would explode from the half-hurt, half-thrill. Whatever was stuck behind his breastbone wanted to get out, and it wanted to get out fast.

But he wouldn't allow it.

Had he felt that way about one of the girls he'd squired around Slashlark – and there had been several – he would have acted with the thought. R'li, however, was at one and the same time an attraction and an obstacle. She was a siren, a female that men refused to name woman. Unhuman, deadly, believed to have all the attributes of the legendary half-animal charmers of the legendary Mediterranean and Rhine, she could not be approached without peril of life and soul. The State and the Church, in their vast wisdom, forbade man to touch a siren.

But State and Church were far-off and shadowy abstractions.

R'li was near and golden-brown flesh and purple-blue eyes and scarlet mouth and glittering hair and magnetic curves. She was look and laugh and bounce and sway and flash and shadow and come-on and get-away and I-know-you and you-don't-know-me.

She broke into his tight-lipped silence.

'Whatever are you thinking about?'

'Nothing.'

'Wonderful! How do you manage to concentrate so fiercely on nothing?'

Her joking helped him regain his balance. His chest quit hurting, and he was able to look R'li in the face. She no longer seemed the most desirable creature in the world; she was merely a – a female who happened to embody – and embody was the right word – embody what a man dreamed of when he dreamed of a – there was no getting away from the word – of a body.

But he had been close to . . . no. Never. He would not even think of it. He must not have thought of it. How could he? A few seconds before that black and aching fire flared up, he had been angry enough to strike her. Then fire on anger had metamorphosed into the shape of desire.

What had happened? Had she cast a spell over him?

Jack laughed, but he would not tell her why when she asked what was so funny. When he tried to blame his feeling on siren's magic, he was not being honest with himself. He was skeptical about sorcery, anyway, though, of course, he never mentioned it. No. She'd thrown no spell. Unless it was the witchcraft any good-looking female could practice without calling in the devil.

Name the thing and let it die. Lust it was called, and it was nothing else.

Swiftly, he crossed himself and swore silently that he would tell Father Tappan about his temptation at the next confession. And told himself that he lied and that he would never say a word of it to anybody. He was far too ashamed.

As soon as he got home and was able to settle things with his father, he'd drive into town and see Bess Merrimoth. He could forget about R'li when he was with a nice lean human girl, that is, if, after such thoughts, his touch wouldn't befoul her . . . No! That was nonsense, he mustn't think like that. He loathed those who went around full of self-imposed guilt and would not allow God or anybody to forgive them. It was a form of self-pity, which, in turn, was a means of getting attention.

Realizing he had to get out of the tightening spiral of introspection, he made an effort to talk again to R'li. She had, he knew, been evading the subject of the dragon. So he asked her about it.

'It's just this,' she replied. 'You really owe your life to us, you know. The dragon told me you were trailing her with intent to kill. Several times she could have circled you and taken you from behind. But she didn't. Her contract with us says that only in case of defense, and as a last resort, may she – '

'Contract?' croaked Jack.

'Yes. Perhaps you've noticed a pattern in her so-called maraudings on the farms around Slashlark. One unicorn from Lord How's estate one week. Next week, one from the Chuckswilly farm. The following, one from O'Reilly's. Seven days later, a beast from the Philippian monastery herd. Then one from your father's place.

'After which the cycle starts again with Lord How, and so on, ending up with the stallion taken five nights ago from your father's pens. Aside from the pattern of rotation, the terms are: No plow or milk unicorns to be taken. No pregnant mares. Only those tagged for the meat market. Dogs and humans avoided as much as possible. No more than four unicorns a year from each farm. Only one dragon to an area. Same contract next year, but subject to alteration if circumstances demand it.'

'Wait a minute! Who said you horstels' – the word sounded as if he spat it – 'could dispose of our property as if it were yours?'

She glanced down. Only then did he realize his hand was on her arm. The skin was so smooth it seemed half liquid, smoother even (he could not help the treacherous thought) than Bess's.

Her eyes flickered down to the withdrawing hand, then up to his flushed face as she said, coolly, 'You forget that, according to the contract your grandfather made with my folks when they agreed to share the farmland, you men were to give us four unicorns a year. That has not been done, by the way, for the last ten years because we horstels have had enough from our own herds to eat. We have not demanded our rights because *we are not greedy*.'

She paused and then added, 'Nor have we said anything to the tax collector about the unarguable fact that your father has been claiming exemption for those four unicorns even though he's kept them for himself.'

Jack was not too annoyed to miss her attachment to the *we* of what human grammarians called the Particle of Ambiguous Contempt.

Jack thought there was a flaw in R'li's explanation of the dragon's raids. If a contract had been made, why didn't they simply take the four unicorns and hand them over to the monster? Why go through the rigmarole of allowing the beast to make her dangerous night forays? The story didn't make sense.

True, horstels seldom lied. But they did now and then. And their adults used child-talk when telling fiction; *she* had used it with him.

That didn't necessarily mean she was lying, for she had taught it to him when they played together as children on the farm, and it was only natural she should continue using it.

Egstaw, the Watcher on the Bridge, was standing on the road, close to the tall round tower of quartz-shot stone that was his home. He was painting on a large canvas supported by an easel.

His wife, Wigtwa, was crouching about thirty yards away on the creek bank. She was skinning a scaly two-legged squamous about two feet long that she'd just hooked from the water. Nearby, three youngsters played in the water. Ana, five years old, could not be distinguished from a human infant of her age except by a very careful scrutiny. That would have shown the beginnings of a fuzz running from the back of the neck and down the valley of the spine.

Krain, a boy of ten, had a backbone that flashed golden when it was at a certain angle to the sun.

Lida, just thirteen, illustrated the next-to-the-last stage of horstel hairiness. Orange-red, inch-long, a roach divided her back and continued to hang a foot beyond her coccyx. Her pubes bore the first intimations of the diamond and the disc. Water-darkened, they, plus the faint swell of breast, hinted at the coming glory of the siren.

R'li gave a delighted shriek at seeing her aunt and uncle and cousins and ran to them. Egstaw put down his palette and brush and trotted toward her; Wigtwa dropped the squamous and knife and raced toward the bridge. Behind her, the children, screaming with joy, splashed through the creek.

All embraced and kissed R'li many times, laughing and crying and hugging her and each other. In the midst of it, she began talking and waving her hands wildly as she tried to compress into a few minutes her experiences of the last three years.

Jack hung back until her uncle came up to him and asked, in English, if he would care for fresh bread and a stein of wine or beer. Later they would have barbecued squamous.

Jack replied he did not have time to wait for the meat. He would take a drink of wine and some bread, however.

Egstaw said, 'You won't be lacking human company either. We have another guest.'

He waved at a man who had just stepped out of the bridge tower. Jack was surprised. Strangers in this frontier county were always regarded with curiosity or suspicion or both; especially one friendly enough with the natives to enter their dwelling.

Egstaw said, 'Jack Cage, meet Manto Chuckswilly.'

As they shook hands, Jack said, 'Any relation to Al Chuckswilly? He has a farm close to ours.'

'All human beings are brothers,' said the stranger gravely. 'However, he and I could probably trace our ancestry back to the original Circassian whose name was, I believe, Djugashvili. Just as I can trace my first name back to Manteo, one of the Croatan Indians who came with the Roanokians. What about you?'

Jack said mentally, 'Damn!' and resolved to quit talking with the fellow as soon as possible. Evidently he was one of those who carried in their heads the whole family tree and who took great pride and much time in leaping from limb to limb and inspecting every twig, every leaf, and the veins and traceries in the leaves themselves. Jack thought it a futile piece of knowledge. All humans could claim descent from each and every one of the original kidnapees.

Chuckswilly was very dark, about thirty, was clean-shaven, and had a long jaw, thick lips, and a large, high-bridged nose, His clothes were expensive: a white felt hat, broad-brimmed and tall-crowned; a jacket of dark-blue werewolf pelt; a copper-studded broadbelt from which hung a copperwood knife and a rapier. His short kilt was linen, white with scarlet pin stripes. Kilts had long been worn in the capital city, but they had not yet become popular in the outlying rustic districts. Calf-length brown boots completed his garb.

Jack asked to see the rapier. Chuckswilly whipped it from its sheath, threw it in the air, and left it to Jack to catch. Smoothly, Jack seized it by its hilt. He did not like the stranger's gesture of trying to catch him off guard and make him look clumsy. Big-city airs, he thought, and shrugged.

The shrug did not escape the keen black eyes, for Chuckswilly's thick lips lifted to expose teeth as unhumanly white as a siren's.

Jack assumed the pose he'd been taught in the Slashlark Academy for Bladesmen, saluted the stranger, and then lunged at an imaginary foe. He shadow-fenced for a while, trying it out until he had its feel. Then he turned the rapier.

'Wonderfully flexible,' he commented. 'Made out of that new Bendglass, isn't it? I'd sure like to get one. I've never seen any around here. But I've heard the Slashlark garrison is going to be equipped with all the newest inventions. Glass helmets, cuirasses, jambs, and shields! Spears and arrowheads, too! And I've heard that they've made a glass that'll stand up to powder charges! That means guns! Though I understand the barrels can only be used a dozen or so times before they have to be thrown away.'

He stopped short at a barely perceptible nod of the stranger's head in the direction of the approaching Watcher.

'Only rumors,' said Chuckswilly. 'But the less the horstels know about it, the better.'

'Oh, I see,' mumbled Jack. He felt as if he'd betrayed a state secret. 'What did you say you were doing?'

'As I was telling Egstaw here,' the dark man spoke smoothly, 'I am one of those fools who like to seek the Holy Grail, the Unattainable, the Never-to-be-found. In other words, I'm a prospector, an iron-sniffer. The Queen pays me to search for that fabulous mineral. So far, as might be expected, I've not seen even a shaving of iron around here. Or any place.'

He cocked his head and smiled at Jack so that big crinkle-flowers grew around his eyes.

'By the way, if you were thinking of turning me in for having entered a horstel dwelling, save your breath. As a Government mineralogist, I'm legally empowered to do so, provided, of course, the Wiyr concerned invites me.'

'I wasn't thinking of any such thing!' said Jack, flushing.

'Well, you should have. It's your duty.'

Cage almost turned and walked away. What an unpleasant fellow! But the desire to save face and to impress the stranger stopped him. As a reply, he whipped out his scimitar and held it up so the sun bounced off it.

'What do you think of that?'

Chuckswilly looked envious and a trifle awed. 'Iron! Let me touch it, hold it!'

Jack threw it up in the air. The dark man caught it deftly by the hilt, thus disappointing Jack, for he'd hoped Chuckswilly would miss it and grab its edge and cut his hand. What a stupid and childish trick! He should be too big to ape city gestures.

Chuckswilly slashed the air around him. 'This would take off the heads! Snip! Snip! What the Queen's men couldn't do if they had weapons like this!'

'Yes, couldn't they,' said Egstaw drily. He watched the scimitar returned to its owner. 'Frankly, I'm very doubtful of any good results if you should find an iron mine. However, as I understand it, the general contract made with the Dyonisan government says that any qualified humans may search anywhere for minerals, provided they get consent from the local Wiyr. As far as I'm concerned, you may go up into the Thrruk Mountains and look.

'But werewolves are numerous there, and dragons are allowed by contract to attack any human they find there. Moreover, if any Wiyr you meet cares to kill you, he may do so without fear of retaliation from his own kind. The Thrruk is, in a sense, sacred to us.

'In other words, no one will hold you back from the mountains. But neither will anyone help you. You understand?'

'Yes, but what about companions? How large a group may go?'

'No more than five. Any more automatically breaks the agreement. I may as well tell you that several times in the past, large bands have illegally gone up into the Thrruk. None were ever seen again.'

'I know. And you say you can't tell me if you Wiyr have found any traces of iron there?'

'Not can't. Won't,'

Egstaw smiled as if he knew he were being exasperatingly mysterious.

'Thank you, O Watcher on the Bridge.'

'You are welcome, O Smeller-Out of Trouble.'

Chuckswilly frowned. Stepping closer to Cage, he muttered, 'These horstels . . . But the day will come.'

Jack ignored him to watch R'li, who had come from the tower. She carried a ball of green soap made of totum fat and an armful of freshly cut softgrass. He couldn't keep his eyes off her swaying hips and the sweep of her horsetail as it swung back and forth like a sensual pendulum in contra-rhythm to the hips. He wanted to watch her bathe in the creek, but he noticed that the stranger was regarding him with narrowed eyes.

'Fear the soulless siren as an abomination. Lie not with her, for she is a beast of the field, and you know what is commanded be done to the man caught with her.'

Jack replied to Chuckswilly's softly spoken question. 'A cat may look at a queen.'

'Curiosity killed the cat.'

'Sharp nose shows sharp brain. Mind-your-own-business gathers money,' retorted Jack, and wondered how silly he could get. Proverb-trading would make you no richer, either.

He walked away to examine Egstaw's painting.

The Watcher followed and explained it in child-horstel. 'That is an Arra showing this planet to the first Terran. He is telling him that here is his chance to get away from all the diseases, poverty, oppression, ignorance, and wars that have scabbed the face of his home-earth. The catch is that he will have to co-operate with the beings that already live there. If he can learn from the horstels, and they from him, then he will have proved he is capable of being allowed to develop in greater directions.

'It is a more or less controlled experiment, you see. Notice the somewhat threatening left fist. That symbolizes what may happen to man, both here and on Terra, if he has not re-formed by the time the Arra return. Man has about four hundred years to found a society that will have co-operation as its basis, not cutthroat hate and aggression and prejudice.

'Man will have on Dare no superior weapons to slaughter the backward natives, as he is doing on Earth. Here almost all the iron and other heavy elements disappeared a millennium before man's coming.

'The ravaged society had been one that used steel and fire and explosives on an inconceivable scale. Wiyr traveled in flying machines, talked across thousands of miles, and did many things you Darians consider to be witchcraft. But this world was blown apart; only a pittance of people were left, though, luckily, the most intelligent. Most of the plants, insects, reptiles, and animals were wiped out by weapons whose nature we do not today know.

'But the Wiyrs created – not rebuilt – a new type of society and a new type of sentient being. The survivors decided they had come close to exterminating themselves because they did not know *what* they were or *how* they functioned. So they determined to find out first and then, if necessary, build a technological society. First, to survive and progress, they would know themselves, *nood stawn*, as we say. Later would come the unveiling of Nature.

'They succeeded. Out of the ravage they formed a world free of disease, poverty, hate, and war – a world that went along as smoothly as could be expected from self-determined individuals. That is, until the Terrans came.'

Jack ignored the remark. When truth and politeness struggled on a horstel's tongue, the truth almost always won.

He looked at the painting closely. He had seen few, since pigments for paint were scarce on this iron-poor planet. He did recognize the Arra, however. The creature had been described enough at school, and he had seen charcoal copies of the original charcoal portrait of an Arra made by the original Cage from memory shortly after the Terrans had been dumped on this world. The Arra looked something like a cross between a man and a tailbear (an 'ursucentaur', Father Joe had called it).

Egstaw said, 'You will notice that, despite the benignity on its great face, it also looks threatening, perhaps sinister. I have tried to portray the Arra as a symbol of the universe.

'This immense and nonhuman creature stands both for the physical, which works best with man if he is not vicious or arrogant, and also for that beyond the material face of things. Many of us definitely feel there are such – should I say supernatural? – powers, though we use that term in a different sense than Darians, that some are powerful but kindly, and that they are likely to use means terrifying but seemingly hostile to men in order to teach them their lesson. If man won't learn, so much the worse for him.

'Don't misunderstand me. The Arra are not supernatural beings. They're as much flesh and blood as you or I. Nor do I believe they work under direct orders from the postulated shadowy Powers. The Arra stands for both the reality we know and the reality behind that. You see?'

Jack saw, but he didn't like the obvious idea that man was a child who had not yet learned the lesson of life and that the Wiyr were to be his teachers.

Chuckswilly snorted and walked away. Egstaw smiled. Cage thanked the Watcher for his explanation and for the bread and wine. He said he'd have to be on his way, though he really would like to stay for the barbecue. He wasn't just being polite by showing reluctance to leave. Every step toward home brought closer the moment of reckoning with his father for having abandoned the shearing and gone hunting with the priceless scimitar.

Deciding he couldn't put off the trip back any longer without admitting cowardice, he whistled to Samson. Chuckswilly had gone on, and he wanted to catch him. The stranger would be better than no company at all. Besides, he wished to ask him if he were going to take anybody along on the iron-sniffing expedition into the Thrruk. He was very curious about what could be found up there.

R'li called after him. He turned to find her walking toward him and wiping her wet skin with softgrass.

'I'll go a little way with you.'

A loud whinnying startled Jack. From around the high stone wall of the far end of the bridge pranced two unicorns pulling a three-wheeled carriage. Chuckswilly was driving. When he saw the two walkers, he reined in his beasts. As usual, they would not quietly obey the driver but insisted on rearing and plunging and whistling rebelliously. Finally, the whip, cutting into their flanks, compelled them to stand motionless. But their long slanted eyes glared as if they would bolt at the slightest sign of weakness in their driver.

Chuckswilly swore and shouted, 'Holy Dyonis preserve me! That we should have to put up with such bundles of nerves and stupidity! I wish we'd brought along the legendary horse when we came here. That, they say, was a splendid animal!'

'If any such thing ever existed,' replied Jack. 'May I ride with you?'

'And I?' added R'li.

'Get in! Get in! That is, if you want to chance breaking your neck. These things are liable to take off across a meadow or through the woods.'

'I know,' said Jack. 'Driving them's bad enough. But you should try plowing with them.'

'I have. You should try hitching a dragon to your plow. They're far stronger and much more co-operative.'

'What?'

'Just jesting, Cage.' Chuckswilly jerked a thumb at Samson. 'You'd better keep him behind us. Otherwise, my team *will* panic.'

Jack gazed speculatively at him. He did not seem like the sort of person who would make a joke about dragons. Or about anything else.

The dark man yelled 'Giddap!' and flicked the woolly backs. The capricious team now insisted on trotting. Their driver shrugged and allowed them to set their own pace. The unshod two-toed hoofs clattered against the dark-gray stuff of the highway.

The iron-sniffer began asking questions about Jack's goals. He replied curtly that he'd finished his studies at the monastery school last winter and since then had been helping his father.

'What about the Army?'

'My father paid the price to keep me out. We couldn't see my wasting my time there. It'd be different if there were a chance for a war.'

R'li said, 'Are you still planning to go to college at the capital?'

He was suprised. He hadn't seen her for three years; he didn't remember saying anything to her about that before she'd left. It was barely possible he had, though, and horstels had long memories.

Or could she have heard about it while she was up in the mountains? The horstel grapevine was far-reaching.

'No, not now. I want to go to school, but not to St. Dyonis. I've become very interested in mental research. Brother Joe, my science teacher, was the one who encouraged me. He told me, however, that the best place for me to go was not to the priestly schools at the capital, but to Farfrom.'

'Why a foreign country?' broke in Chuckswilly loudly. 'What's the matter with your own land? With your own teachers?'

'I want the best,' Jack replied harshly. He was sure now that he didn't like the dark man. 'After all, it was a priest that told me about Roodman. He's supposed to know more about the mind of man than anybody else.'

'Roodman? I've heard of him. Isn't he on trial for heresy?'
R'li said, 'He was, but he was found not guilty.'
Jack's eyebrows rose. Their grapevine, again . . .
'I heard they freed him because his accusers disappeared under mysterious circumstances. There was talk of black magic, of demons snatching away those who wanted to burn that sorcerer.'
R'li asked, 'Has anybody ever seen a demon?'
'It's the essence of demons that they're not seen,' said Chuckswilly. 'What do you think of it, Cage?'
Uneasily Jack wondered if the fellow could be an agent-provocateur.
He said cautiously. 'I've seen none. But I will say I'm not afraid to be alone on the nightroad. Werewolves and mad tailbears are the only things I look out for.
'And mad men, too,' he added, thinking of Ed Wang. 'But not demons.'
Chuckswilly snorted like a unicorn. 'I'll give you a word, my hayseed friend. Don't let anybody hear you talk like that. You might be able to get by with it in this frontier settlement. But a statement like that would be bomb powder in the older parts of Dyonisa. There are a million ears to hear and a million tongues to carry your words to the gray torturers.'
'Stop the carriage!' shouted Jack. He yelled at the team, 'Whoa!'
They halted. Jack jumped out and walked around the vehicle to the driver's side. 'Get out, Chuckswilly. I don't allow anyone to call me a hick. If you're going to shove your lip around, you've got to back it up with your arm.'
Chuckswilly laughed, white teeth showing against the swarthy skin. 'No offense, youngster. My speech, I'll admit, is rather free. But I meant what I said about your getting into trouble. However, let me remind you that I am on the Queen's business. I don't have to take up challenges – sword, axe, fist, or otherwise. Now, jump back in, and we'll be on our way.'
'Not me. I just don't like you, Chuckswilly.'
He turned and began walking down the road. Chuckswilly's whip cracked. Hoofs drummed, and the wooden wheels clattered.
'No hard feelings, young fellow,' the driver called out as he flew by.
Jack didn't answer. He took two more steps. And stopped. The siren had not been in the carriage.

He wheeled and said, 'You didn't have to get out just because I did.'

'I know. I do pretty much what I want to.'

'Oh.'

Why should she want to be with him? What were the thoughts beneath that swarm of lovely red-gold? She wasn't hanging around because she liked his big brown eyes, he was sure.

A flutter in the shadows of a tree trunk caught his eye. Without saying a word to her, he walked to the tiny creature that was beating its half-formed wings in a vain try at flying. Samson leaped at it, but he stopped short and nosed it. His master did not bother to tell him to leave it alone; he knew the dog was too well trained to bite without his permission.

'A bluebeard fledgling,' he called back to R'li.

He held up the minute flying mammal with its fringe of blue-blackish hair around the monkeylike face.

'Fell out of its nest. Wait a minute. I'll put it back.'

He removed his weapons belt and shinnied up the trunk. As it was a spearnut tree, it lacked branches for the first thirty feet. He hugged the smooth bark, legs and arms embracing it tightly, while one hand held the tiny bunch of fur and wings away from the bole. Thus he was forced to press hard with his wrist, using it in place of the occupied hand. It was a very tiring and awkward posture, but he had climbed all his life.

Not stopping to rest, he inched up steadily until he reached the first branch. Then he hooked an arm over it, swung his body up with a jerk, clamped a leg over another branch, and in a short time had deposited the fledgling with two of his brothers. They barked small-throated welcomes. The parents were nowhere to be seen.

When he got down, he saw the siren looking at him with shining eyes.

'You have a tender heart beneath that angry mouth, Jack Cage.'

He shrugged. What would she say if she knew he'd helped bury her cousin, Wuv?

They resumed walking. She said, 'If you want to go to Farfrom, why don't you just go?'

'As the eldest son, I'll inherit most of the farm. My father depends on me. He'd be heartbroken if I were to give up my future here and study under a man he considers to be a black magician, a mind doctor.

'Besides,' he ended lamely, 'I haven't the money I need to live on while I'm studying.'

'Do you quarrel often with your father?'

He decided not to take offense at that question. Horstels weren't expected to have human manners. 'Often.'

'Over that?'

'Over that. Father's a rich farmer. He could send me away for four years. But he won't. Sometimes I think I'll leave anyway and work my way through Roodman's Academy. But my mother gets sick when I talk of going. My sisters cry. Mother would like me to be a priest, though she never stops to think that the Church is likely to send me far away and that I'd seldom return.

'It's true I could, as a priest, study psychic science by applying for entrance in the Thomistic College. But there is no guarantee I'd be admitted. And even if I did get in, I'd be under strict control in research. I'd not be a free agent, as I would under Roodman.

'Something else. If I became a priest, I'd have to marry at once. I don't want a wife and children. Not just now. Maybe later.

'Of course, if I entered the Philippian Order, I'd be a monk. But I don't want that, either.'

He paused for breath. He was astonished that he had picked himself up, so to speak, like a pitcher, and poured himself out. And to a siren, at that.

But, he comforted himself, he often spoke his problems to Samson. She was in the same class as the dog. And the results were also the same. She would not report what he'd said to his parents.

'Perhaps if you found something that would free you financially, you might be able to decide.'

'If I'd taken the dragon's head, I'd have had enough. Lord How's reward, plus the Queen's bounty, would have made it.'

'Was that why you were so angry when you found out we had made a contract with it?'

He nodded. 'One of the reasons. I – '

'If it weren't for those agreements, human territories would be ravaged,' she interrupted. 'You've no idea how terrible or how invulnerable they are. They could devastate a farm in one night, kill all the animals, and uproot the houses.

'Moreover, if it weren't for the contract, you'd be dead

now. The dragon said she could have surprised you half a dozen times.'

His woodsman's pride was stung. He barked out a four-letter word that had spanned many centuries and many light-years unchanged. 'I can take care of myself! I don't need any siren to tell me how!'

He walked on silently, hot and tired and irritated.

'How would you like a loan?' she said. 'Enough to take you through school?'

It *was* a day of shocks.

'Loan? Why? With what? You horstels don't use money.'

'Let me put it this way. First, we know this man Roodman. We think his psychology is correct, and we'd like to see it spread. If enough humans become psychically cleansed of their aberrations, they may be able to ease the terrible tension between them and us and avert the war that is otherwise inevitable.

'Second, you may not know it, but the Wiyr have long had their eye on you. They know that you are – consciously or unconsciously – sympathetic to us. They want to develop that.

'No. Don't protest. We *know*.

'Third, we are trying to get representation in your Parliament, human representatives to sit in the Houses for us. If we do, we think that someday, after you mature, you would make a good delegate for the Slashlark County Wiyr.

'Fourth, you need money to go to college. We'll give you what you want. All that's necessary is that you make the usual verbal contract. My father, the Blind King, may be the recorder, if you wish. Or if not, anybody else will do. And if you insist, you may have a human lawyer draw up papers – for your convenience. We, of course, will have nothing to do with that.'

Jack said, 'Wait a minute! You've not even seen your folks. How do you know what they're planning for me? And how did you get the authority to offer me a loan?'

'That's easily explained. But you wouldn't believe me if I told you. As to authority, any adult has it. I'm an adult.'

'Then quit using child-talk! I'm not an infant. And – and how can I know these things unless I ask?'

'True. Now, what's your decision?'

'Why – that'll take time. Your offer is something I never heard of. It has many angles that have to be considered carefully.'

'A horstel would make up his mind at once.'

He bared his teeth and shouted, 'I'm not a horstel! And there is the meat of the matter. I'm not a horstel, and the answer is no! Why, if I took money from you, do you know what the people around here would call me? *Dog-eater!* I'd be ostracized; my father would kick me out of his house. Nothing doing. No!'

'Not even a loan just to go to Roodman's Academy? No strings attached?'

'No!'

'Very well. I'm going back to my uncle's. Goodbye until we meet again, Jack Cage.'

'Farewell,' he growled, and he began walking down the road. Before he'd gone two yards, he heard her call.

He turned, pulled around in spite of himself. She'd sounded so urgent.

She had her hand up in a sign for silence. Her head was cocked. 'Listen. Hear that?'

He strained his ears. He thought he could make out a very low rumbling to the west. It wasn't thunder; he was sure of that. And the sound faded out now and then.

Samson was a yellow statue, pointed to the west. His throat-rumble echoed that in the forest.

'What do you think it is?' he asked.

'I'm not sure.'

'The dragon?' He drew the scimitar.

'No. If it were, I wouldn't investigate. But if it's what I think it is . . . '

'Yes?'

'Then . . . '

She walked into the dark shadows thrown by the tall spearnuts, towering copperwoods, and tangled vines growing overhead. He followed, curved steel in hand. They zigzagged perhaps a mile as the bear ambles, perhaps a quarter-mile as the lark flies. Several times he had to cut away a barricade of vines or stingbushes. It was the thickest and most impenetrable growth he'd ever seen. Though close to the farm, it seemed never to have been explored.

Finally she stopped. An arm of sunlight had pushed through a hole in the green ceiling and spread its fingers over her red-yellow hair. Haloed, she stood there, listening, and Jack, behind her, forgot about their quest long enough to admire her. If he were a painter, like her uncle . . . !

Suddenly the noise came to life close by. She started, and she and the light seemed to break into pieces. The next he knew, she had glided into the shadows.

When he caught up with her, he whispered, 'I've never heard anything like that. It sounds like a giant trying to sob and gurgle at the same time.'

She said softly, 'I think you're going to get to go to Farfrom, Jack.'

'You mean it's the dragon?'

She didn't answer but leaped over a fallen log. He reached out his free hand and clutched her arm.

'How do you know it's the same dragon. Maybe it's one that's not made a contract?'

'I didn't say it was a dragon.'

She was standing close to him, her naked arm and hip brushing his.

He strained his eyes to make out shapes in the gloom.

'Maybe it's a mad tailbear. This is the season. And you know what one bite means.'

'Oh!' she breathed, and she moved closer. Unthinkingly, he gave way to his protective feeling – later he excused himself by saying she'd reminded him of his younger sisters – and put his arm around her waist.

Her eyes were half closed, so he could not see the light in them. Thinking back on that particular moment during the succeeding days, and he did much of that, he remembered the slight smile on her lips. Were those indentations the marks of amusement? And if he could have read her eyes, would he have seen that their expression matched her lips? That she was not at all frightened but was laughing at him?

Or would there have been a third emotion?

Whatever he thought later, he had no doubt at that instant. He forgot about the mysterious danger ahead. His arm squeezed her waist, pulling her to him. He was breathless. Human or not, there was no woman as beautiful as she or as desirable.

The peculiar rumble brought him back to his senses. Dropping his arm, he stepped up ahead of her where she could not see his face.

'You stay behind,' he said in a choking voice. 'I don't know what it is, but it sounds very large.'

'It also sounds very sick,' she added. Her voice held the same breathlessness as his.

He pushed through the vegetation.

Somewhere, hidden in the green tangle but near, a behemoth retched.

Tony burst in.

His mother, sisters, and brothers were half raised from their chairs and staring at their father with astonishment, rage, fear, or barely hidden amusement. The master of the house was the only one yet sitting; he was as if struck by a club. Nor could he have been more paralyzed. His half-bald head was covered with thick, yellow, and steaming egg-pudding; a viscous cataract flowed down his face and sank into his beard.

Lunk Croatan was a wax dummy. The bowl remained upside down in his hands. His brown face was opened wide: jaw hanging, postrils flared, eyes round.

There was no telling what might have happened next, for Master Cage was not a man to take such things laughingly, even though accidental. That is, if it were an accident, for in the following moment Lunk's eyes closed, his eyes wrinkled, his nostrils pinched, and the thin lips curved into an idiotic grin. Giggling, he blew out a cloud of wine.

Wherever Walt's skin showed beneath the yellow flood, it was turning red. The volcano was evidently ready to blow.

Then Tony chortled, 'We're rich! Rich!'

Only that word could have sidetracked his father's gathering wrath. He turned to Tony and said, 'What? What did you say?'

'Rich!' squealed his youngest. He ran to Walt and grabbed his hand. 'Come on. Jack's outside! Stinking rich!' He laughed wildly. 'I mean it. He's stinking, and he's wealthy!'

His mother could endure no more. She rushed past Tony and bumped into her husband just as he was rising. Though he outweighed her by a hundred pounds, he was off balance enough so that the impact toppled him back into his chair.

At any other time, Kate would have been very flustered. Now she only said 'Oh!' and left him speechless and red on his chair.

Behind her came her flock, pushing and shoving. Lunk stepped aside for them, picked up a large napkin from the sideboard, and began wiping off his master's face and beard. He did not apologize; he only giggled.

Walt swore, tore the cloth from the servant's grip, and stomped out onto the front porch.

It was a curious scene for a homecoming. Everybody was standing around Jack, but no one, not even his mother, would go close to him. Some, especially his sisters, were beginnning to turn pale. And all were paying more attention to what Jack had placed on the porch table than they were to him.

The moment Walt stepped outside, he stopped. He dragged in a deep breath, coughed, and then almost strangled. Now he knew what Tony's words meant.

If the father was astonished, the son was not less so.

'Great Dyonis!' said Jack. 'What happened to you?'

'That fool Lunk,' growled Walt, as if that explained it. 'Never mind.' He pointed at the mass on the table. It was round and large as a man's head, gelatinous and gray, and it gave the illusion of always quivering, as if it were alive and shaking with terror because it had no skin.

'That's a gluepearl? Right?'

'Yes, Dad. While I was on my way home, I heard a sicktree retching in the forest.'

'Sicktree? *Close* to home? Man alive, how did we ever miss it? Right on our doorstep, so to speak. And the horstels?'

'I imagine they knew all about it. They just didn't want to say anything about it.'

'Isn't that like them? All the money that sicktree represented, and they were keeping it for themselves.'

'Not exactly.'

Jack hated to tell his father about R'li and how he was obligated to her. He was going to explain later. Anyway, she'd refused to split the money he would get for the rare perfume base. It was her contract right to claim half of it, but she'd insisted it was all Jack's. Nor would she explain why. Not at that time, at least.

Jack had been reluctant for it to stand that way. He could not help thinking of her murdered cousin. His blood had scarcely been washed off before she was leading Jack to the costly forest prize. It was no accident they'd found it, he was sure of that. On the way home he'd analyzed the steps leading to its discovery. He knew why she had been determined he should have all the money that would come from its sale. One way or the other, her kind was going to see that he went to Farfrom. And when he came back, he was scheduled to stand in Parliament as their speaker.

That's what they thought.

'You see,' he explained to his father, 'the Wiyr know what

they're doing. It takes thirty or more years for a sicktree to develop a mature gluepearl. If it was known one was around here, how long do you think it'd be before some merchant or highwayman would be chopping the tree down to dig out the concretion, even if it were only half grown? Thus, the full value wouldn't be realized, and there'd be no more future gluepearls. No. They knew what they were doing.'

'Maybe so,' said Walt. 'But, son, what a fabulous stroke of fortune that you should be going by just when it was retching. Fabulous!'

Unhappily, Jack nodded.

Walt looked at the scimitar at his son's side. He opened his mouth as if to reproach him for having taken it. Then he shut it.

Jack could read the thought in his head. If his son had not taken the blade without permission and gone off on that quest, he would not have found the gluepearl. Even now, the gray mass might be lying on the ground at the foot of the tree, undiscovered and rotting, three thousand pounds worth, rotting, rotting away . . .

Suddenly, as if awakening, Walt started, looked at Jack, and grinned. 'Son! You stink! But no matter. It's a good stench; no more welcome one.'

He rubbed his hands; a curd of pudding fell off his nose. 'Lunk, you and Bill grab that table and carry it to the strongshed. Lock and bar it well and bring me the key. Tomorrow, we'll drive into town and sell it.

'Ah, Jack, if you didn't stink so, I'd hug and kiss you! You make me happy. Think, son! You've far more than enough to buy Al Chuckswilly's farm. You can now ask Bess Merrimoth to marry you. When you two come into your full inheritance, you'll have five farms – her father has three – all large and rich. Plus the Merrimoth tannery, warehouse, and tavern. Plus the most beautiful girl in the county. Ah, those red lips and black eyes! I'd envy you, Jack, if I'd not already married your mother.'

He glanced hastily at his wife and said, 'What I meant, Kate, was that Bess is the most beautiful virgin. You, of course, are by far the best-looking matron roundabout. Anybody may see that.'

Kate smiled and said, 'It's been a long time since you said anything like that, Walt.'

He pretended not to have heard her. He dug his big fingers

into his beard and pulled fiercely at the roots while he said, 'Look, boy. Maybe, instead of the farm, you could bribe some of the officials at court and buy your way into a knighthood. Then you could work your way up to a lordship. There's no telling what an ambitious man can do here. This is frontier territory; you're a Cage. There'll be no holding you back.'

Jack grew angry, but he kept his face composed. Why didn't his father treat him as a man and ask him what he wanted to do? It was his money, wasn't it? Or it would be in two years, when he came of age.

Lunk and Bill returned. The house servant handed Walt the big glass-and-copper key to the stronghouse. Walt gave it to his wife. Suddenly he bellowed, 'All right, Kate! And daughters! Into the house. And don't look out the windows. Jack is going to be as naked as a satyr.'

'What do you mean?' asked Jack in some alarm.

Kate and the older girls giggled. Magdalene said, 'They are going to get rid of that stink, Jack.'

Lunk came from the house with several large washrags and big bars of soap.

'Close in on him, boys,' ordered Walt. 'Don't let him get away.'

'Hey! What do you think – ?'

'Tear off his clothes! They have to be buried, anyway . . . They'd make a maggot puke . . . Grab his arm . . . Off with his trousers. Jack, you crazy unicorn, you kicked me! Take your medicine like a man!'

Laughing, choking, struggling, they picked up the writhing, naked body and bore it to the watering trough in front of the barn.

Jack fought and yelled and howled; then he was plunged head first into the water.

Three mornings later, the barking of dogs and the gaggle-gurgle of cocks awoke Jack. He sat up and moaned. His head was a balloon of ache. His mouth tasted like the scrapings of a wine barrel. Last night had been long on joy and short on sleep. The cellar had been raided; two kegs of the oldest fermented totum juice had been broached.

Walt Cage had been strangely reluctant to take the glue-pearl into town. It was as if the sight of the quivering jelly whipped his nerves into ecstasy. Originally, he'd planned to drive into Slashlark at dawn of the next day. When he got up, though, he spent thirty minutes in the strongshed, contemplating it. Afterward, he announced that this good fortune would have to be celebrated. He astonished everybody by saying they would have a party tomorrow, shearing or no shearing.

Lunk drove away with the invitations; Bill Kamel shrugged and set out to do what he could with his reduced shearing gang; the women began baking and scrubbing and talking about what they'd wear. Walt himself, though he wielded a pair of shears, was not as much help as he should have been. Every now and then he would walk away, unlock the strongshed, and look again at his treasure.

The evening of the following day, the guests drove in. Wine and beer flowed from the always-open spigots; two unicorns turned on spits. All insisted on seeing the fabulous 'pearl.

Walt was in the clouds – the clouds being formed half of pride and joy, half of wine fumes. He shouted that the frequent trips to the stronghouse were shrivelling his nostrils and crisping his tongue and that he was absorbing so much of the stench that one more inspection would make him as expensive as the sicktree's fruit itself and as much sought after.

He'd take the visitor by the hand and lead him into the stronghouse and hold him there while the unfortunate sightseer cried out to Walt to let him loose, that he would lose meat and wine and add to the stench if he could not get out at once.

Master Cage would laugh and open his grip on the other's arm. Or he would slam the door shut and yell that he was going to keep the guest locked in all night to guard the treasure. The trapped one would beat on the door and demand, for the love of God, that Walt quit jesting and please release him. The very air was enough to make a man's lungs gangrenous. When the door was opened, the man would reel out, clutching his throat and turning green-and-white-spotted. All would laugh and thrust steins at him and tell him to dip his nose until he got rid of the perfume.

Mr Merrimoth, his widowed sister, and his daughter arrived. Bess, tall and dark-haired, black-eyed and high-cheekboned, red-lipped and round-bosomed, had been permitted to come – even though the hour was late.

Jack was glad to see her. His skin was tight with wine by then. Normally, he did not care to drink so deeply. Tonight was different. Only by befogging himself could he overcome the self-consciousness resulting from the odor that still clung to him even after the scrubbing.

Perhaps that was why he insisted on showing his discovery to Bess. Close to it, she would not be able to smell him. The two went down the tree-shadowed path alone. Bess's aunt for once did not accompany them.

Her father raised his eyebrows when he saw them saunter off, and he looked at his sister. After all, Jack had made no formal request to bundle with her. When he took a step after them, the aunt laid a detaining hand on his arm and shook her head to indicate there were times when a girl had a right to be alone with her beau. Mr Merrimoth obeyed the superior wisdom of the female. Nevertheless, as he accepted another glass from the house servant, he wondered what sensitivity it was that enabled her to know that tonight Jack would probably take the first step to be put in the yoke . . . no . . . he meant holy matrimony.

The two saw the quivering ball. By then Jack was sick of its sight. Bess gave the conventional shrieks of horror and protestation and asked how many pounds the thing was worth. He answered swiftly and rushed her out and back up the path.

At that moment the *broomm*! *broomm*! *broomm*! of drums and the blowing of horns came down wind from the northern meadows. Suddenly the horizon blazed with fires. Jack muttered, 'R'li is home.'

'What did you say?' said Bess.

'Would you like to watch the horstel's homecoming?'

'Oh, I'd love it,' she answered, squeezing his hand. 'I've never seen one. Would they mind?'

'We won't show ourselves.'

As they walked over the fields beneath the bright light of the huge moon, he felt his heart thudding. Bess? Wine? Both?

The drums sank, muted; lyres rose and traveled across the moonlight in spectral images of sweet notes; a panpipe thrilled. And R'li's voice lifted, a golden tower, building upon itself, higher and higher, swiftly and incredibly changing, going up, ever different, yet always R'li, creamy yet fiery, sweet yet dangerous, essence of siren, of woman, shifting, liquid.

A big-bodied stringed instrument softly crept into the background, throomed, then fell silent as that last note hovered, steadily beating its wings against the current of time and endurance of flesh. Held, would not fall, would not. Until the listeners' hair rose on the backs of their necks, their skins prickled, and their nerves seemed naked to the air.

Vanished.

Bess clutched his arm and murmured, 'God, that was wonderful! No matter what you say about them, you have to admit they can sing.'

He took her hand and led her on. He didn't trust himself to speak.

Afterward, he had rather vague memories of looking through a bush at the celebration around the fires. They watched a ritual dance, in which R'li took part, and then an improvised dance. During that, the siren disappeared into a hole at the base of the nearest cadmus. She came out shortly after and Jack, watching for her, saw something else that startled him.

A face was peering out from the flickering shadows within the entrance. Though distant and smudged by the alternation of light and dark, the heart-shaped outline, the big eyes, and the swelling lower lip were plainly those of Polly O'Brien.

As soon as he was certain of that, Jack took Bess by the hand and pulled her away. He told her their folks would begin to wonder why they were away so long. Only half willing, excited by the music and the naked bodies swirling around the fires, she walked slowly, leaning on him. She chattered on and on of this and that; he didn't hear much of it because his head was swirling at the sight of R'li and at the discovery of the refugee. Around and around they went in his mind, until he became aware that Bess had stopped him and was looking up at him, eyes closed and lips pursed for a kiss.

Abruptly he tried to forget his problems by kissing her passionately. He would abandon all thoughts about those other two females; they were not really any concern of his; what he needed was a woman who was all right with the world he knew. Marriage, home, babies, and all the rest. That was the way out.

By the time they got back, she had promised to marry him. They decided not to tell anybody their intentions. After the spring plowing was over and everybody would be available for a big celebration, they'd announce their engagement. A secret it would be, though, of course, Jack would ask her father if they could bundle. Although termed a prelude to engagement, bundling really meant affiancement, for few couples dared brave public opinion by breaking up afterward. Legally still a virgin, the girl actually was considered to be *non intacta* thereafter. Her chances for getting some other boy as a husband were greatly reduced; her best policy was to move to some place where it was not known she'd bundled. And that was so impractical as almost never to be done.

So their secret was in name only. Jack thought it was silly, but like most males, he went along with the woman.

He noticed that as soon as they returned, Bess whispered something in her aunt's ear. Both turned to stare at him when they thought he wasn't looking.

The party lasted until close to dawn. So it was that Jack had about two hours' sleep and woke with a swelling head, a foul taste, and an even fouler temper.

He rose, dressed, and went to the kitchen. Lunk was sprawled out, asleep, on a pile of werewolf hides behind the stove. When Jack prodded him in the ribs with his toe, Lunk didn't event grunt. Deciding it'd be easier to make a pot of wakeup himself than to rouse the servant, Jack started a fire. He put on a kettle of well water and measured out three spoonfuls of the dried and shredded leaves of the totum tree. While he was feeding the dogs, the shreds would loose their stimulating essence in hot and brown liquid.

Returning from his chore, he found that somebody had drunk all of the wakeup. He kicked Lunk in the ribs. Lunk said, 'Ughh!' and turned over. His face was sweat-shiny from the heat of the stove.

Jack kicked again. Lunk sat up.

'Did you drink my wakeup?'

'I dreamed I did,' the servant replied thickly.

'Dream! Well, dream that you're getting up and making me some more. That's what I get for trying to help you.'

As he had orders from his father to wake him early, Jack knocked on his parents' bedroom door until his mother was aroused. She, in turn, shook her husband until he got out of bed.

After the three men had a light breakfast of steaks, liver, eggs, bread and butter and honey, cheese, spring 'onions', beer, and wakeup, Lunk left to harness up a carriage team, and the two Cages began walking across the farm.

Walt said, 'It hurts my pride to have to accept anything from a cadman. But I don't suppose I'll be able to argue R'li out of her decision. You know their proverbial stubbornness.'

He whistled awhile, rubbing his middle finger against the side of his nose. Unexpectedly, he stopped in the middle of a bar and clamped his son by the shoulder.

'Tell me, Jack. Why did this siren renounce her share?'

'I don't know.'

Walt's fingers dug. 'You're sure? There's nothing – personal?'

'What are you getting at?'

'You're not . . . ' Walt seemed to be searching his mind for a word that would not be too foul, and came up with 'consorting with her?'

'Dad, how could you? With a siren? Why, I hadn't seen her for three years. And we were alone only a short time.'

The fingers fell away. 'I believe you.'

Walt passed a hand over his red-shot eyes. 'I – I shouldn't even have asked that question. I wouldn't have blamed you if you'd struck me. It was a terrible thing to say. Only, you must understand, son, there's more of that sort of thing going on than you think.

'And I know how seductive they can be. Twenty years ago, before I was married . . . well, son . . . I was tempted once.'

Jack didn't dare ask if he'd succumbed.

A few minutes later, they paused to watch a group of youthful satyrs whose spine and loin hair was just beginning to grow thickly. They were down on their hands and knees and crumbling the soil of the field between their fingers. From time to time they laid their ears against the ground, as if they were listening. Intermittently, their fingers drummed hard against the crust.

Their supervisor was a tall adult whose tailhair was so long he'd plaited it into a large tight ball that brushed against his calves as he walked.

'Good morning,' he said amiably in English.

His eyes were clear, his face was unpuffed, he showed no signs of the night-long revel. 'Scarcer than a horstel's headache,' ran the proverb.

Walt said, 'O Listener to the Soil, how go things?'

The two talked gravely and wisely as two old farmers who respected each other. They discussed the texture of the earth, its moisture content, and the day they would start plowing. They talked of manures, of rotations, predatory animals, and dry and wet spells. The Listener said he'd 'heard' there were many earthworms under the crust, and he told of a new, larger, and more efficient type of worm that had been bred in some far off Croatanian cadmus.

He agreed with Walt that they should have a good crop of 'corn.' The man, however, was pessimistic about the raids of lark, barefox, tailbear, and sexton. The Listener laughed; they would pay their tithe to Mother Nature's retainers and let it go at that. Unless the tax was too high, in which case the Hunters would reduce the local population of vermin.

He concluded by saying that his sons, the Testers of the Thunder, were up in the mountains trying to locate the pulse of the weather-to-be. When they returned, he would discuss their findings with Walt.

After they left him, the elder Cage said, 'If they were all like him, we wouldn't have any trouble.'

Jack grunted. He was thinking about their designs on him.

The farm was broad and sprawling. There were many things Master Cage thought it necessary to check up on. So that it was not until two hours later that the ivory-white cones of the Wiyr dwellings shone in their eyes.

Even after nineteen years, Jack was fascinated. His father had forbidden him, as a child, to go near them. To Jack, that was equal to an order to loiter around them. The result had been that he knew as much about them as anyone could who'd never gone down into one. He was very curious about what went on beneath the ground. Once, he had almost asked one of his horstel playmates if he could visit. A fear of the consequences had stopped him. Not only would the human penalties be heavy, but the stories he'd heard about what happened to those who took sanctuary had sucked away his courage. Now he no longer believed those old wives' tales. Nevertheless, he could not overcome the prohibition of human authorities.

Cadmus Meadow (every farm had a Cadmus Meadow) was a broad field carpeted with green and red ruggrass, a plant hardy enough to grow despite steady trampling from bare feet. Scattered unevenly, a dozen thirty-foot-high fang-shaped structures of some bony material projected from the meadow.

Cadmuses, they were called, after Cadmus, the mythical founder of Thebes, the hero who had sown the dragon's teeth and reaped a harvest of warriors. The first Earthmen had named them correctly, for when the Terrestrials had grown populous enough to feel strong, they had attacked the nearest native community. And out of the cadmuses had swarmed an overwhelming number of warriors, who repelled the invaders, overcame them, and disarmed them.

Right then and there the aborigines, if they had done to the Terrans what the Terrans had planned on doing to them, could have settled the man-cadman problem once and for all. For the strangers from a distant star had plotted to massacre the natives and take over their underground homes and enslave the survivors.

Fortunately for the Terrans, they were given another chance. A contract was made. A hundred years of peace passed.

Then the sons of Dare, trying to live up to their name, had broken their word and declared war on the natives within their territory. Only to find that the Wiyr knew no national boundaries and that every adult on Avalon was ready to march upon the strangers and crush their inferior numbers in a day.

Caught between external pressure from the cadmen and the seething internal turmoil among themselves, the nation of Farfrom exploded.

A revolution overthrew the reigning dynasty of the Dares. Farfrom became a commonwealth governed by a citizens' committee. A new contract was made. The policy of cadmus-sanctuary for criminals and political refugees was established. Capital punishment was abolished. Witches were no longer to be burned.

The minority of Catholics and Socinians, unhappy with certain other developments, took advantage of the turbulence to march off to distant parts of the continent of Avalon.

Isolated from other men behind a high range of mountains, the Socinians abandoned religion, clothes, houses, and even language. They went completely native.

Thirty years after the martyed Dyonis Harvie IV had founded the state that bore his name, Dyonisa was split by civil war. A political-religious-social schism resulted in two contending parties: the Church-in-Abeyance and the Church-in-Expediency.

The Expedients won. Once again, the dissatisfied took the best move to be made in a frontier country. Led by a Bishop Gus Croatan, they packed up and went to the large peninsula, which later became a new nation.

Both Expedients and Abeyants crowned a new church leader, the *caput*, in each of their respective capitals, and claimed that he was the leader of the only true church.

Horstels smiled and pointed at Farfrom, which also had a man who denied that anybody but himself was the vicar of God on the planet Dare.

This history ran through Jack's mind as he approached the meadow. It was interrupted as they stopped before the nearest shiny-white cadmus. O-reg, the Blind King, was standing before the entrance and smoking a roll in a long bone holder.

'Greetings, O Owner of the House. Good fortune, O Finder of the 'pearl.'

The Blind King was red-haired and tall and thin. He was not blind, and a king in that almost anarchic society was unknown. But he held a position that gave him a title whose meaning was long lost in antiquity.

The older Cage asked if he could speak to R'li.

'There she is,' said O-reg, pointing past him to the creek. Jack turned, and his pulse thudded, for the siren stepping from her bath was a vision of beauty. She sang softly as she swayed closer, then stopped, and kissed her father. O-reg put his arm around her narrow waist, and she leaned her head against his shoulder as she talked with Walt.

Now and then her eyes strayed to Jack, and she smiled. By the time his father, redfaced, had given up trying to get her to accept her share, or at least to say *why* she wouldn't, Jack had decided to have a little talk with her.

When Walt began discussing the shearing with the Blind King, his son beckoned to her to come away with him. Out of earshot of his father, Jack said, 'R'li, you knew that that wasn't any bear making that noise. Why did you grab me as if you were frightened? And hang on? You weren't afraid, and you knew it was a sicktree. Right?'

'Right.'

'Then why did you do it?'

'Don't you know, Jack?' she replied, and she walked off.

The elder Cage delayed taking the 'pearl into town for one more day. The frequent trips he made to the stronghouse had now made him a laughing matter among the family and hired help. He acted as if the gray quivering jelly were part of his own flesh. Selling it would be like cutting off a piece of himself for money.

Jack, Tony, and Magdalene, the least-restrained of his children, made so many jests that last day that he must have become aware they thought his actions peculiar.

The morning of the fourth day after the 'pearl was brought home, the two oldest male Cages and Lunk and Bill Kamel drove away from the farm. They wore helmets of copperwood and leather strips, cuirasses of bone strips, and heavy gantlets. Walt drove; Jack and Bill carried repeater crossbows; Lunk sat on the box containing the 'pearl, a javelin in his hand.

Despite their fears, they made the twelve miles to the county seat without unusual incident. No robbers rushed from the forest and demanded the treasure. The sky was bright and cloudless. Slashlarks flew by in large flocks. Their four-noted song filled the air. They fluttered on green-yellow bat-wings. Now and then, one unfolded the huge red claws that had given them their name. Once, a female swooped so close that Jack could see a tiny ball of fur clinging to the mother's belly. The fledgling turned its flat face and looked with black fleck-eyes at the men.

Once a tailbear ambled onto the road. The unicorns, always nervous, almost stampeded. Walt and his son both pulled on the reins and managed to hold them back until the monster, ignoring them, disappeared into the woods.

They passed seven farms. The area north of the capital was not well populated, and it was doubtful if it would be in the future. So far, the cadmen had refused permission for more settlers, claiming that these would upset the ecological balance.

The Mowrey farm was the last they went by before arriving at the bridge that spanned Squamous Creek. The Watcher leaned out of his tower window and waved. Lunk and Bill returned his salute. Jack noticed that his father scowled and kept the reins tight-gripped, so he decided it would make trouble if he waved back.

After they crossed the bridge and began following the road along the place where Squamous Creek emptied into Bigfish River, they saw no more Wiyr. Unless business required their presence, the latter stayed away from large towns.

The top of a steep hill gave them their first glimpse of Slashlark. Its back was to a large hill. Its face was to the broad river. Unimposing, it consisted of a long main street and a dozen side streets. Commercial and government buildings, taverns, and the ballroom lined the highway. The residential houses were on the subsidiary lanes.

Fort Slashlark squatted at the southern end of town. Its glittering red log walls housed a hundred soldiers.

Many boats lined the wharves. Sailors worked on the decks, loading furs, leather, candled lark eggs, logs, the first of the wool crop, and box on box of winter totumballs. Those not working sat in the taverns and argued with off-duty soldiers and looked at the women.

The military police made sure that all they did was look. Bored, the police were hoping for a chance to bang a club over a riverman's hard skull.

The Cages drove through the crowded street. Walt jerked at the reins and shouted at a wagon full of beer barrels that was at right angles to the traffic. Its driver was sweating and swearing in his efforts to separate his team; the four unicorns were kicking, biting, horning, and squealing for some unknown cause. Abruptly, a hoof lashed out, and the driver fell on his back, stunned.

When the unfortunate man (only one of many annual victims of the unpredictable beasts) had been dragged to the sidewalk and the team had been led off to one side, the Cages drove on. Then an urchin dashed in front of them, and again their two animals tried to run away down the crowded highway.

Jack and Bill jumped down and seized the stallions by the harness and hung on until they decided to stop. After which, they led the snorting and trembling creatures to the hitching bar in front of the Queen's House, a government building.

There the agent for a perfume company weighed the gluepearl, locked it up, and wrote out a receipt. He apologized because he was unable to pay out the four thousand pounds it was worth. The revenue collector would have to witness the transaction and take the 'Queen's bite' on the sum. She had big teeth. She'd leave only two thousand on the plate.

Though he would still be well off, Jack resented losing so much. And his father rolled his eyes upward and swore to high heaven that the taxes were ruining him, that he'd be better off if he sold his farm and moved into a big city and went on the dole.

It was then that his son got an inkling of the true reason Walt had tried to get R'li to keep her share. Being a cadman, she would not have to pay a tax on her half; Jack's tax, calculated on a sliding scale, would have been cut by two-thirds.

Later, Jack had no doubt, his father would have suggested to R'li that he might take the money she got from the sale. That way, he could have beaten the Queen out of about three-quarters of her due. It was a clever scheme, but the horstel stubbornness had thwarted Walt. No wonder he'd displayed even more than his normal amount of vehemence against them.

On leaving the Queen's house, they met Manto Chuckswilly. The dark man greeted them cordially and asked if they'd care to have a drink on him at the Red Horn. He said that there were quite a few of the local citizens gathered at the tavern.

'Oh, by the way, Jack, your cousin, Ed Wang, will be there. He's especially eager to see you.'

Jack's heart flicked. Was this a meeting of the HK? Was he about to be invited – or, rather, told – to join?

He looked at his father. Walt would not meet his eyes.

Jack said, 'I'll be there. In a little while. I have to see Miss Merrimoth first.'

'That's all right, son. But when you get there, turn over a half-hour glass. As soon as it's run out, get back here.'

Walt glanced at Chuckswilly, who nodded that that was agreeable to him.

Thoughtful, Jack walked away. He'd asked Lunk how long the prospector had been in town. The servant, who seemed to know everything about people's movements, had replied that Chuckswilly had come to Slashlark about two weeks ago. During that time, he'd introduced himself to everybody worth being introduced to. He had spent much time at social affairs and very little in preparing for an expedition into the Thrruk.

As far as Jack knew, Chuckswilly had not met his father. During the time previous to his going after the dragon, he was sure his father had not gone into town. But he might have done so while his son was up in the foothills. Jack didn't know; he'd forgotten to ask Lunk about that. Whatever had happened, it seemed obvious that Walt and Manto Chuckswilly were acquainted.

The Merrimoths lived in a large two-story house set on top of a hill at the outskirts of Slashlark. Next to Lord How's, it was the finest in the county. Someday, if Jack married Bess, he would own it, plus the Merrimoth farms, tannery, warehouse, and the gold in the bank. His wife would be the best-looker for miles around. He would be the envy of all the young men.

Yet, an hour later, he left the house, dissatisfied and disgruntled.

Nothing was different. Bess was as beautiful and sweet and amusing as ever. She had sat on his lap and kissed him until, after a decent interval, her aunt entered the parlor. Then, whispering, she had discussed plans for the marriage.

He'd not felt the excitement he should. Nor had he the courage to say anything about his idea of going to Farfrom. Several times he'd opened his mouth, but each time he'd choked back the words as he realized that if he proposed putting off the marriage for four years, he would kill the happy light in her eyes.

Not that he'd set any definite date for the wedding. But in Slashlark you just took it for granted that you married as soon as possible and began having children. Asking her now to sit at home alone while he spent forty-eight months in a city three thousand miles away, would be impossible. Nor would he want her to do that.

Just before he left, it occurred to him that he could take her with him, that perhaps she might even like the idea of going to far-off places. He felt a momentary elation. It passed as he remembered the close bond between father and daughter. Mr Merrimoth would probably raise so much cain that she would rather stay home than antagonize her father.

In which case, Jack thought, that would mean that she loved her father more than him.

Why not ask her and find out?

He would. Not just now, though.

Later, when he'd more time to think about it, and when her aunt could not listen in on them.

Or was that sheer dodging the issue?

Honest even though it hurt him, he had to admit that he lacked the guts to bring his plans into the open.

So it was that he began walking faster toward the Red Horn. He needed a drink.

Jim Tappan, owner of the tavern, nodded when Jack entered. 'Back room,' he said.

Jack knocked on the door. Ed Wang opened it. Instead of swinging it back to let Jack in at once, he held it half-open and stuck his head around the edge. Evidently he didn't want those behind him to see that he was saying something. Judging by the babble coming from the rear, however, he need not have feared he'd be overheard.

He talked under his breath. 'Listen, Jack. Don't give me away about Wuv, will you? They know he's dead. I told them. But my story isn't quite as you'll remember it.'

Coolly Jack said, 'I'd be a fool to commit myself that way. I *will* see how things are going before I speak up. Now, out of the way, Cousin.'

Ed glared. Jack pushed in on the door. For a second, Ed looked as if he were going to put his shoulder to it and keep Jack from coming in. Then a thought, visible as the strange look that flickered over his broad face, made him change his mind. He stepped back. Jack, without having hesitated in his stride, brushed by him.

Within, about thirty men were seated on hard and bare benches against the walls. Twenty were around a huge oval table in the center of the room. One was Walt, who lifted a hand to point out an empty chair next to his.

Most of those in the room paused in their talking to watch him. Their eyes, behind lifted steins or burning pipes, were unreadable. Jack was chilled. He supposed they might have been discussing his fitness as a candidate.

The list of men there read like a high-society register of Slashlark County: Merrimoth, Cage, Al Chuckswilly, John Mowrey, Sheriff Glane, Cowsky the lumberman, Dr Jay Chatterjee, Ed's father Lex, Knockonwood the fur trader.

Lord How was not present, nor was Jack surprised to find him missing. The old fellow was often spoken of as being too fond of the cadmen on his estate, and it was hinted that in his younger days he had had a depraved fancy for sirens.

However, young George How was here. He raised a stone cup to Jack in silent salute and drank. The beer slopped out over his thick lips and ran down his two chins.

Jack smiled back. Despite the fellow's self-indulgence, he was a good companion. He had but one bad fault. When in his cups, which was often, he would be the best of drinking comrades. At the beginning. And then, somewhere during the evening, he would suddenly jump on the tabletop, his eyes staring, his lips slobbering, and begin shouting his hatred of his father. When that was exhausted, or when his friends quit listening to him, he raged against them, accusing them of many actual and imagined faults. He then would leap at them, fists swinging.

Those who knew him were prepared and jumped on him, held him down, and poured water on him until he sobered up. Several times, however, they'd been forced to knock him on the head or punch the wind out of his baggy stomach. He bore two close and parallel dark lines on his high forehead, scars given by friends who'd swung their pacifying steins a little too hard.

No matter. Next day, he didn't remember what he'd done.

He greeted the ones he'd attacked as if nothing had happened.

As Jack sat down, he saw that Manto Chuckswilly was the only man standing. And seated next to him were two soldiers from the fort: Sergeant Amen and Captain Gomes.

The iron-sniffer said, 'Jack Cage, this is a rather informal meeting. There will be no candles lit, no masks worn, no mighty oaths sworn.'

His lips curved ironically.

'So you may act as you wish, not as a young initiate who should be properly respectful and awed toward his elders.'

Several of the older men looked blankly at him.

'Ed Wang has told us how he was attacked by Wuv and how he was forced to kill him. He also told us how you discovered him shortly after. Will you please describe, in your own words, what happened?'

Jack spoke slowly and distinctly. When he was through, he looked at Ed. His cousin's face had the same expression as when Jack had caught him above the corpse.

'So then,' said Chuckswilly, 'the satyr had three wounds in his back. Master Wang, you didn't mention that.'

Ed jumped up and said, 'I stabbed him when he turned to run away. Like all horstels, he was a coward. He knew I was overpowering him, and he knew I was going to kill him.'

'Hmmm. Jack, how large was Wuv?'

'Six feet two. Weighed about sixteen stone.'

Chuckswilly ran his gaze up and down Ed's short figure. He said, 'I hate the Wiyr, but I do not allow myself to be blinded by realities. I've never seen a cowardly satyr. Nor have I ever heard of an authentic case of one attacking a man. Unprovoked, that is.'

Ed's face twisted and became pale.

'Sir, are you calling me a liar? Those are dueling words, sir.'

'*Sir*,' replied the dark man, 'sit down. When I want you to stand, I'll ask you.

'Meanwhile, let me remind you gentlemen of something. The HK is no play society. We are in this for blood. We have chosen you, the cream of this county, as the nucleus of the local chapter.

'Mark, I said *chosen*, not invited. I need not say what will happen to any who refuse to join. We are taking no chances. And we are, despite our seeming informality, a military organization. I am your general; you will unquestioningly obey my orders. Otherwise, you will suffer due punishment.

'Now – ' He stopped, frowned and then growled at Ed.

'Sit down, sir!'

Ed's neck was trembling so much his head shook. 'And if I don't?' he grated.

Chuckswilly nodded at Sergeant Amen. The soldier, a huge man, brought his hand up from under the table. It held a knobheaded stick. The knob struck Ed in the mouth. He fell back, knocking his chair over, and lay on the floor. Blood ran from mangled lips; after a minute, he rose and spat out three teeth. Tears flowed from half-shut eyes while he pressed a handkerchief against his mouth.

'Now sit down, Master Wang. Please remember that in the future there will be no killings unless *I* give the word. And don't worry or chafe because you are getting no immediate action. The day will come when you'll wade in blood.'

His swarthy, big-nosed face swung toward the others, and he said, 'If there should be one who does not agree with me, he may report me to the authorities. Sheriff Glane and Captain Gomes are at your disposal. You will not even have to leave the room to denounce me.'

Uneasy laughter ran around the room. Merrimoth stood up and pointed a stein at the prospector.

'Mister Chuckswilly, you're a man after my own heart. Hardheaded, hardfisted, and with your feet on the ground. You know when to strike and when not to. A health to you, and to the HK.'

Chuckswilly picked up a stein and said, 'To us, sir.'

He drank. The others rose and drank. They did not sound very loud, however, as they echoed his words.

'Now, Ed, would you care to join in the toast?' said the dark man. 'There should be no hard feelings – you're well off. When I was organizing at Old City, I had to kill a man because he insisted on settling a personal grudge with a satyr. The fool couldn't see that the long view is the best.'

Ed removed the kerchief. Slowly he lifted a stein and dipped it to his leader. In a voice mangled as his mouth, he said, 'To the damnation of all horstels, sir.'

Chuckswilly said, 'That's a good boy, Wang. One of these days you'll be thanking me for having knocked some sense into your head. And now, if you please, perhaps you'd like to tell us what you told me before the meeting?'

Ed's voice shook as he began, but as he progressed, it regained some of its old ring.

'It's this. Mr Mowrey's son Josh knows how I feel – felt – about Polly O'Brien. Yesterday he came to me and said that the night she ran away, he was walking home from the Cospito farm. He'd been bundling with Sally Cospito and it was very late, about four in the morning. The moon was still up; he was hurrying because he was nervous about werewolves. They've been seen recently, you know.

'He was just about to turn in at his father's farm, when he heard a carriage rumbling over the bridge at Squamous Creek. Curious as to who'd be up and driving at that hour, he stepped behind a bush. And he was glad he did, because a masked man was driving and a hooded woman was beside him. And in the back seat were two satyrs. He couldn't tell, of course, who the humans were. But one of the horstels was Wuv. He's sure of that.

'Josh also said that though he couldn't see the girl's face too well under that hood, he'd swear she was O'Brien. I think it's obvious she took sanctuary in the cadmus on the Cage farm. And I think that – '

'It's time for you to sit down,' cut in Chuckswilly.' Mr Cage, from the way you've been puffing away on your pipe, you must have something to say.'

Walt rose and said hoarsely, 'I knew nothing at all about her being on my farm. Believe me – '

'Nobody suspects you,' said Chuckswilly. 'She could have been on anybody's property. As a matter of fact, knowing the cadmen, I'm surprised they didn't hide her on the Wang farm. But your place, Walt, is the most logical as it's the closest one to the mountains.'

Ed rose again. 'If that's true, Polly will be taken away some dark night into the Thrruk! Don't you think before that happens we should raid the cadmuses and drag Polly out and burn her for a witch? That'd show the horstels they can't get away with just anything they want to, and it'd show the humans that there's hope for them, that there's a group that's willing to do anything to carry out justice!

'Why, we could mask ourselves and go armed with bombs and burning oil. Catch them asleep, slaughter them, burn out the cadmuses. And destroy their goods, too, their crops and trees and wine and meat – '

'Sit down!' thundered Chuckswilly.

Jack's father heaved his bulk up and began pounding on the table. 'Mr Chuckswilly! I protest! If we were to follow Wang's plan, it would mean much more than the massacre of my horstels. It would mean my ruination! My farm would be destroyed; I'd be a poor man! How would the attackers be able to distinguish between the cadmen's property and mine? Not only that, but – '

'Please sit down, Mr Cage.'

Walt hesitated, then he lowered himself. He breathed so heavily his face was red, and he pulled hard at the roots of his beard.

'You are correct,' said Chuckswilly. 'Your ruination as property owners may be one of the results of HK-Day and a minor one at that.

'No – quiet, please,' he said as a babble broke out. 'Allow me to explain.'

He turned to the wall behind him and pulled down a large map of Avalon. He used his dagger as a pointer.

'Each one of these crosses indicates a group of cadmuses. The circles mark the centers of human population. Where there are large towns or cities, there are few cadmuses. Humans now outnumber the horstels twelve to ten.

'But in the rural areas, the horstels outnumber us. That means that on HK-Day, if things are left the way they are, they'll have the upper hand in areas such as Slashlark.

'We don't intend to leave it that way. On The Day, simultaneously with night attacks of our Society on each cadmus, mobs of city people, inflamed by speeches, free liquor, and promises of loot, will pour out of the urban areas and into the rural. They'll be armed, we'll see to that. They'll be in a killing frenzy.

'Once the battle is launched, the Government will be impelled to back up the citizens. Especially since many officials are HK members. And the Queen, I'm sure, is looking for just such an action to break the cadmen contracts and order the Army to attack.

'The HK is international. We've allied ourselves with heretics so we humans may act as one. Once the horstels are wiped out, we'll take care of the heretic problem.

'Now, Master Wang, you wanted action at once. You'll get it. We've planned a raid, but not on cadmuses. It'll be on an Army wagon train coming by the Black Cliff road to the fort here. The wagons will hold the new Hardglass flintlock barrels, bullets, bombs, and a glass cannon, which will be very handy to blast open the hard shells of the cadmuses.

'Also, there is a wagonful of flame projectors. These shoot a chemical that, if poured down entrances, will either burn or strangle all life underground.'

Jack thought. If the Government was not secretly preparing for war and if it was opposed to the HK, why was it shipping weapons that seemed specifically designed for a cadmus siege?

The answer was obvious.

' – meet at ten that night at the Merrimoth warehouse and decide on the details of the raid. The raiders are going to have to do something that will go against their grain. They'll have to disguise themselves as satyrs. That is so the Queen may have an opportunity to blame the horstels.'

He chuckled, and he was dutifully echoed.

'Now, Mr Cage, the point that bothered you. You fear the HK will get out of hand and destroy or loot everything in sight. You are half right. The city mobs will do just that. You see, you gentlemen live far from the cosmopolitan areas. You don't realize how destitute, how hungry, how desperate the poor are. Penned in their drafty and dirty firetraps, run over with noisy hungry brats, resentful, they hate the wealthy human as much as they do the cadmen. More, really, because they blame the aristocracy and the rich for their situation and they have scarcely any dealings with the horstels.

'So, the day that they spill out of the cities, they won't be satisfied with just slaying the Wiyr and robbing them. Tasting blood, uplifted by the lack of restraint, they'll seize the chances given by the inevitable chaos and turn on those who have what they've never had.

'Now, now' – he held up his hand to still their protests – 'the HK was set up for more than one reason. Our primary goal, of course, was to organize and launch the attack. But almost as strong was the desire to hold down the mob, to preserve law and order. In short, to protect ourselves against an antagonist almost as dangerous as the cadmen – the manpack.

'Consequently, only half the Army will be used in the cadmus attacks. The other half will be held in reserve to act as a police force and get the crowds back into the cities once they've done their work. So, gentlemen, please don't be surprised at anything that happens on HK-Day. There'll be lives lost, perhaps some of yours. Houses and barns will be burned, crops trampled. Mean beasts will be cooked on the spot by the hungry and frenzied poor. Fortify your houses, lock up your stock.

'But do not look so dismayed. After all, it's worth it to rid yourselves once and for all of the soulless beasts of the field. Victory is worth nothing if easily won.

'Now, any questions?'

Again Jack's father stood up. He leaned on rigid arms; his fists pressed into the tabletop. Sweat ran down his cheeks and into his beard, and his voice was strained.

'This consequence was unseen by all of us. Especially one point. If I understand you correctly, every horstel will be killed. That isn't what I thought would take place. I thought enough would be slain to show them who their masters were, And then the survivors would keep on working the fields, but as our slaves. So there'd be none of this nonsense about sharing the fruits of labor with them.'

'Not at all!' Chuckswilly stabbed with the dagger to emphasize his argument. 'There *must* be no shilly-shallying. Every cadman *must* be killed. Would you replace one problem by another? If we did as you suggested, we'd still have noplace for the city folk to go. How could we allow them to settle in the country if horstels still lived in the cadmuses? No. Once the Wiyr are gone, the landless will be moved, quietly, orderly, and slowly into the less-inhabited areas. There they will become farmers.'

'But . . . but,' choked Walt, '*they* don't *know* anything about farming. They'll *ruin* the soil, the orchards, the herds. They're ignorant, lazy, dirty, shiftless. We'll never get the co-operation from them that we get from the horstels. Nor will we be sure about dividing the shares at the end of a season. Their word is no good. The result will be that we'll be dragged down to their level. We'll be as poor as they!'

'Possibly true,' said Chuckswilly. 'In a way, that is. You gentlemen will not have to give away part of your land, or share it. Your property will remain yours. The immigrants will become hired help, dependent on you. They will be, in a sense, tailless horstels. But not as independent.

'You'll have trouble, of course, breaking these people in, teaching them to love farming as their predecessors did. They'll make mistakes. Your lands will, for a while, suffer. But, eventually, something like the former production will return.'

'What about the people left in the cities?' asked Mr Knockonwood. 'We've enough trouble now feeding them. Won't they starve during the interim?'

'No more than before. Why? Because you'll have only half the population to feed that you once had.'

'What? Why?' ran around the room.

'Why? Think, gentlemen. So far all you've seen is a rosy future – the cadmen out of the way and all the wealth yours. Not so. Has it occured to you that the horstel is aware of what's going on? That he'll fight even more fiercely than the human, because he knows it's a war of extermination? That they could have their HK-Day date set, too? Perhaps earlier than ours, so they could overwhelm the rural population and then march on the cities? That HK could mean, just as well, Human Killer?'

Jack looked at Chuckswilly with increased respect. Brutally cynical though he was, he was also honest, intelligent, and realistic. That was more than you could say for the rest of the men in the room.

Chuckswilly said, 'I'll tell you at once, so the weakhearted may steel themselves, that we expect to lose half our forces.'

'Half?'

'Yes – a terrible price. But though I hate to say it, it's a good thing. It'll make more room. It'll be a couple of generations before Avalon begins to get crowded again. It'll also kill the threat of revolution from the cityman, who, as you gentlemen know, has been making the Queen uneasy for some time.

'No, it'll be a bloody, bitter time. Gentlemen, prepare yourselves.'

Tony brought Jack's lunch. He found his big brother standing in the middle of the field, hanging onto the plow handles and cursing the team.

'Every time they see a shadow they try to run away. I've been here since dawn, and I've done nothing but baby these brutes.'

'Gee, Jack, I know,' said Tony. 'Why don't you eat your lunch now? Maybe you'll feel better afterward.'

'It's not me. It's those beasts. Man, what I'd give for the legendary horse! There, they say, was man's best friend. You could lie down in the shade, and he'd do all the plowing by himself.'

'Why don't you hitch men to the plow? Dad says the first men here did that.'

'Tony, when corn is first planted, it's finicky. It has to be buried deep, very deep. Otherwise the roots don't take hold.

'Dad says our "corn" isn't like what they had on earth. He says that this stuff is a weed that the horstels bred into a plant that could be eaten. But when they did so, they couldn't keep it from being delicate.'

Jack unhitched the team and led them to the creek. He said, 'I understand the unicorns we use now are only a dwarf species. Once, there was a big brother the horstels used for plowing. He was smart and easygoing, like a horse.'

'What happened to him?'

'He was wiped out, like most of the big animals, in a single day. Or so they say. That was the day all the iron on the surface of Dare exploded in one big bang. Boom! And just about killed every living thing there was.'

'Do you believe that?' asked Tony.

'Well, miners and prospectors have dug up the bones of many animals that aren't living now. And you can see the ruins of big cities, like those near Black Cliff, to show that something catastrophic did level them. So maybe it's true.'

'Gee, that was a thousand years ago, too, so Father Joe says. Jack, do you actually suppose the horstels could fly then?'

'I don't know. Anyway, I wish that when all that iron went up into the air, it had spared some good plow beasts.'

'Why don't you hitch up a dragon?' said Tony.

'Sure,' said Jack. He chuckled and began to eat his lunch.

Tony said, 'I read about St. Dyonis converting a dragon. He used him to plow up a big stretch of land.'

'Oh, you mean the story about the time he and his disciples fled Farfrom and came here? And the horstels agreed he and his descendants could inhabit all the country they could circle in one day with a plow. And he fooled them by hitching up this Christian dragon and circumscribing our present nation.'

'Yes, that's it. Wonderful, wasn't it? I'd like to have seen the look on those horstels' faces.'

'Tony, you shouldn't believe everything you hear. But I'd like to have one of those monsters. I bet they could draw as deep a furrow as you wanted.'

'Jack, did you ever see a dragon?'

'No.'

'Then, if you never saw one and you should only believe what you see, how do you know there is any such thing?'

His brother laughed and playfully poked him in the ribs. 'If there isn't, what's been stealing our unicorns?'

Jack looked past his brother. 'Besides, a siren told me she'd talked to the very one that's been raiding our pens. In fact, here she comes now. Ask her if it isn't so.'

Tony grimaced and said, 'Guess I'll be going back, Jack.'

Absently his brother nodded, his attention on the swaying figure approaching. She was carrying a tear-shaped vase.

Tony narrowed his eyes, curled his lip, and slipped off through the trees.

'Hello, Jack,' said R'li in English.

'Hello,' he answered in child-talk.

She smiled as if she saw something significant in his using that tongue. He glanced at the amphora she was holding by one of its handles.

'Going to get some honey?'

'Obviously.'

Jack looked around. No one in sight. 'I'll go with you. The plowing can wait. I'm afraid if I went back just now, I'd be tempted to kill those beasts.'

She hummed the tune to the latest song to reach the county. '"Hitch your dragon to a plow."'

'I wish I could.'

He removed hat, jacket, socks, and boots and began splashing creek water on himself. The siren stuck the sharp end of the amphora into soft mud. She waded into the creek and sat down.

'If you weren't so body-conscious, you could do the same,' she teased.

He glanced around and said, 'It does seem ridiculous. When I'm with you, that is.'

'I'm surprised to hear you admit that.'

'Well, I didn't really mean it. Men need clothes, but it's all right for horstels to go naked.'

'Ah, yes, we're animals . . . who have no souls – whatever those are. Jack, do you remember when we were children, and you used to sneak down to the pool and swim with us? You didn't wear pants then.'

'I was a kid!'

'True, but you weren't as innocent as you pretend. We used to laugh at you, not because you were nude, but because you thought you were so terribly wicked and because you were so obviously delighted with your sense of sin.

'Your parents had forbidden it. If they'd caught you, your beating would have been something to remember.'

'I know. But when they told me I couldn't do it, I had to. Besides, it *was* fun.'

'*Then* you weren't really convinced you should be ashamed of your body. *Now* I think you are. You've allowed others to convince you.

'But then,' she added, 'I can understand why your women put on garments. They use them more to conceal their defects than to enhance their beauty.'

'Don't be catty.'

'I'm not. I think it's the truth.'

He stood up and put on his hat and picked up his clothes. 'Before I go, R'li, tell me this, will you? Why did you give me all claim to the 'pearl?'

Rising, she waded up to him. Each drop of water on her breasts gleamed like a little glass universe with a tiny sun imprisoned in its center. Streams fell from the soaked tresses of the horsetail and splashed upon the sand. She spread the long hairs along her left arm and held them up to the light. Shimmering veins of yellow and red ran with sun.

Her purple-blue eyes looked up at his brown eyes. Her right hand made the familiar gesture toward him. It stopped. He glanced down at it. His hand reached out and took hers.

She didn't pull back. She followed the gentle but firm insistence of his hand and came into his arms.

A week later, the Army wagon train was raided. It was nine in the evening when the HK put on satyr costumes. Their disguise would fool no one in a strong light, nor any who looked closely in a weak light. They weren't worried. They were dressing so mainly to give the Queen's men a chance to accuse the local cadmen.

When they approached the Full Glass Tavern, they found it blazing with light. Indoors, the soldiers were tossing off steins or rolling dice. The wagons were lined up behind the barn. A sergeant was supervising the hitching up of fresh teams. He did not even look up when the first of the raiders stepped from behind the barn.

Overpowering the men on duty was easy. The fake satyrs rushed from the darkness. They surrounded the surprised privates and silenced them, encountering amazingly little resistance. Or, thought Jack as he gagged one of the fellows, was it so amazing?

No roar of discovery came from the inn, despite the unavoidable creak and groan of axle, the snort and clatter of beast, and the rumble of wheel. Once on the road, the raiders threw aside caution and lashed out at the teams. Only then did the tavern door burst open and men, still with steins or money in hand, stagger out to shout and curse.

Jack thought they were poor actors. Their oaths were weak, and he could have sworn he heard several bellow with laughter.

All in all, during the long dash back, he felt anything but brave and daring. He was disappointed because he had not had to draw his Bendglass rapier. Recently he had wanted to strike out at somebody or something. A gray and heavy mass was riding his back, and though he squirmed and kicked, he could not get it off.

Even during his infrequent meetings with R'li, he could not be altogether free of that smoldering rage. Too many of their words were like those of the first time he and R'li had kissed.

He remembered them well. He had gasped out that he loved her, he loved her, and he didn't care who knew it, who knew it.

He'd strained her to him and swore he meant it.

Right now you do, yes. But you know it's impossible. Church, State, Folk bar you.

I won't let them.

There's one way. Come with me.

Where?

To the Thrruk.

I can't do that.

Why not?

Leave my parents? Break their hearts? Betray the girl I'm promised to? Be excommunicated?

If you *really* loved me, you'd go.

Ah, R'li, you say that so easily. You're not a man.

If you went over the mountains with me to the valley you'd have more than just me. You'd become what you'll never be in Dyonisa.

What's that?

A *complete* man.

I don't understand you.

You'd become more balanced, more psychically integrated. The unconscious part of you would work hand in hand with the conscious. You'd not be chaotic, childish, out of tune.

I still don't know what you mean.

Come with me. To the valley where I spent three years going through the rites of passage. There you'll be among people who are whole. You're a ragged man, Jack. That's what the word *panor* means in our language as applied to humankind. The ragged. The collection of pieces.

So I'm a scarecrow. Thanks.

Be angry, if it helps you. But I'm not insulting you. I mean that you don't know your powers. They're hidden from you. By others, and by yourself, yourself playing hide-and-go-seek with yourself. Refusing to see the real *you.*

If you're so – whole – why love me? I'm – ragged.

Jack, potentially you're as strong and complete as any horstel. You could, in the Thrruk, become what you should be. Any human may if he'd tear down that barrier of hate and fear and learn what we so painfully took centuries to do.

And give up all I've got now to do it?

Give up what needs to be given up. The best, the good, keep. But don't decide what is the best until you've gone with me.

I'll think about it.

Do it now!

I'm tempted.

Walk off. Leave the animals tied to the tree, the plow in its furrow. No goodbyes. Just walk off. With me.

I – I can't. It's this way . . .

Please don't make excuses.

Since then, he couldn't rid himself of the feeling that he'd turned back from a path to many glories. For a while he'd tried to convince himself that he had uttered a *Retrocede, Sathanas!* In a few days he was honest enough to tell himself he lacked courage. If he really loved, as she had said, he'd throw aside all to go with her. Forsaking all others, cleave unto . . .

But that applied to marriage, and he could never enter into holy matrimony with her.

He loved her. Did a man in robes have to say words over them? He must think so, for he hadn't gone with her. And she had said that the test of his love was whether or not he'd go with her.

He hadn't.

Therefore, he didn't love her.

But he did.

He struck the wagon seat with his fist. He did!

'What the hell you doing that for?' said young How, sitting next to him.

'Nothing!'

'You get the maddest over nothing,' chuckled How. 'Here. Take a nip of this.'

'No, thanks. I don't feel like it.'

'Your tough luck. Well, cheers. Ahh! By the way, did you notice that Josh Mowrey wasn't with us?'

'No.'

'Well, Chuckswilly did, and he was raising hell about it. Nobody knew where he was. Or at least they pretended they didn't. But I know.'

Jack grunted.

'Aren't you interested?'

'Vaguely.'

'Man, do you feel bad! I'll tell you, anyway. Ed Wang detailed Josh to watch the cadmuses on your farm!'

Jack came alive. 'Why?'

'Ed thinks Polly hasn't left there yet.'

How chuckled and uptilted the flask. He lashed the woolly backs of the unicorns, and when the wagon had gained speed, shouted above the noise, 'Ed's as stubborn a young'un as there is. He and Chuckswilly'll clash again.'

'Chuckswilly will kill him.'

'Maybe. If Ed doesn't slip a copperwood into his ribs. He is acting humble now, but he remembers those lost teeth.'

'Who're we fighting? Horstels? Or each other?'

'Difference of opinion must be settled before you can have a plan of action.'

'Tell me, How, whose side are you on?'

'I don't care. I'm just waiting for the day the big fight comes.'

He took another long swallow and then looked at Jack. Jack wondered if How meant to attack him. He'd seen that tight-lidded expression before.

'Want to know something, Jack? HK-Day is going to see a lot of property change hands. Horstels and loot-crazy humans are going to . . . uh . . . dispose . . . of some people. When that day comes . . .'

He lifted the flask again and said, 'I may become Lord How soon. Of course, grief-stricken, I'll erect a monument to my poor old father, struck down in the bloody turmoil of The Day.'

Jack said, 'No wonder your father thinks he's whelped a fat, stupid, good-for-nothing hound.'

'Watch your tongue, Cage. When I'm Baron How, I'll not forget my enemies.'

He threw the empty flask away. The reins were loose in his hands, and the unicorns, sensing the loss of control, slowed down.

'You think you're so damned intelligent, Cage, I'm going to show you you're not. A little while ago, I lied when I said I didn't care who became top dog in the HK. Heeeh! I always lie. Just to mix people up. Anyway, I know something you don't. About that crazy Wang and that big-eyed piece O'Brien. And that arrogant commoner, Chuckswilly, too.'

'What's that?'

How shook a finger and waggled his jowls. 'Not so fast. Beg.'

How reached into his coat pocket and brought out another flask. Jack gripped him by his collar and jerked him closer. 'Tell me now, or you'll wish you had!'

How gripped the flask by its neck and raised it to strike Jack. Jack chopped against How's bull neck with the edge of his hand. How fell over backward into the wagon, where he was seized by those riding there.

Jack picked up the reins and called back, 'Is he dead?'

'Still breathing.'

Some of the men chuckled. Jack felt better. When his hand had lashed out, it had seemed to discharge much of his repressed fury. The only thing that bothered him was what How had been hinting at.

During the six miles from Black Cliff to Slashlark, the teams were not spared. Jack wondered how they could keep up their pace. By the time they reached the county capital, they would be foundered. And after that they'd have to take a mile detour around the town so the wagons wouldn't be seen. That'd make seven miles, after which they'd have to pull the wagons another seven to the Cage farm. There the wagons would be taken into the barn, and the weapons would be buried under a mound of last year's hay. But would the unicorns hold up?

A half mile out of Slashlark, Chuckswilly ordered a halt. It was then that Jack, like any of the raiders, found he wasn't in on all the planning.

Men, holding torches, stepped from the forest, unhitched the blowing, foam-specked beasts, and harnessed fresh ones. Chuckswilly ordered the raiders to strip off their satyr costumes and put on their clothes.

While they were changing, How crawled out of the wagon. He rubbed his neck and blinked in the torchlight.

'What happened?' he asked.

'You fell and knocked yourself out,' somebody said.

'Wasn't I talking to you, Jack, when it happened?'

'Yes.'

'What'd I say?'

'Your usual drivel.'

'Ha! Ha!'

How quit frowning and looking uneasily at Ed, who'd been standing near by. How grinned and slapped Ed on the shoulder. 'See, Ed! It's all right.'

'Shut your mouth,' growled Ed. He turned and walked off into the darkness.

Jack gazed speculatively at his back. His cousin had that crazy wild look. What was he up to?

The wagon train started again. It passed the stretch of road that curved to the west of Slashlark. Abruptly the range of hills that blocked their view of town sloped away to a plain. They came back to the main highway, the one that followed the Bigfish until it ran into Squamous Creek. There, two hundred yards south of the bridge, the wagon stopped.

Chuckswilly said, 'Here's where most of us go home. The drivers will go on to the Cages' and will sleep there tonight. I'm staying there, too. We'll need some extra men, however, to help unload.'

Details arranged, the men not going on slipped away into the night. Those who lived nearby walked; those whose homes were distant got into carriages that had been waiting all night.

The dark man drove the lead wagon. How the second, Wang the third. Jack did not know who the other drivers were.

The bridge rumbled. The men looked to see if the Watcher would awake and stick his head from a window of the tower. They breathed easier when they'd passed the tall stone structure without a sign that those within had been disturbed. At that moment, a lantern flashed from the creekbank. The Watcher was walking toward them, a long slender pole over one shoulder and a wicker basket hung from his side. It was the men's bad luck that the hórstel was just returning from an all-night fishing trip.

Jack turned to stare behind him. Wang had stopped his wagon, holding up the procession, and was jumping off. He carried a glass-tipped javelin.

Jack tore the reins from How, halted the beasts, and shouted, 'Hey, Chuckswilly!'

Chuckswilly also stopped. When he saw what was happening, he howled, 'You fool! Get back on your seat and get going!'

Wang yelled shrilly. Not at his chief. At the satyr. He threw the javelin without breaking his stride.

Awm dropped the lantern and pole and fell to the ground. The javelin shot over his head into the night. Immediately, Awm jumped up and threw his lantern. As Wang was running forward, knife in hand, and could not dodge in time, the lantern bounced off his head. Wang went down. The glass of the lantern broke; oil spread in a flaming pool; it licked at the head of the unconscious form. The Watcher disappeared into the blackness of the trees.

'Ah, the bloody fool!' said Chuckswilly. 'I ought to let him burn.'

Nevertheless, he grabbed Ed's feet and pulled him away from the fire.

Ed sat up. He held his hand to his mouth. 'What happened?'

'Bloody, blasted dunderhead! Why'd you attack him?'

Unsteadily, Ed rose. 'I didn't want any horstel witnesses.'

'And so now you've one for sure. Wang, I gave no orders. Do I have to knock out every tooth in your head?'

Ed replied sullenly, 'I think Awm's done that.' He removed his hand from his face and revealed a bloodied mouth. Two teeth came out, and he wiggled a third, loose in its socket.

'Too bad he didn't kill you. Consider yourself under arrest. Get back in your wagon. Turk, you drive it. Knockonwood, watch Wang. If he does anything out of the way, run him through.'

'Yes, sir.'

A door slammed. The men looked at the tower. Sounds came as of a bar being shot through a slot. Voices floated to them. A torch lit up a slit-like second-story window.

Ed said, 'While we've been standing here, Awm has sneaked around and gotten home! We'll never take him now!'

The windows in the third, fourth, and fifth floors blazed and then became dark again as the Watcher climbed the spiraling stairs. The sixth remained lighted. Presently against the moon, a long rod was pushed up from the roof.

Jack couldn't determine the color, but he guessed it was made of the expensive copper. From time to time, he'd seen those poles extended from the Watchers' homes or from the cadmus cones. What they were, he didn't know, but he supposed they were used in the horstels' black magic.

Seeing one come up now, like the horn of a demon, made him uneasy. Wang was close to panic. His eyes bulged, and they swiveled from side to side.

Chuckswilly said, 'Enough damage's been done. Let's roll.'

He turned to go.

Ed stopped over and picked up a fist-size rock. Before Jack could do more than cry a protest, Ed had leaped for the chief's back.

Chuckswilly must have had the sensitivity of a horstel, for he'd started to turn back even before Jack yelled. His hand was darting for his rapier hilt. The rock caught him on his temple, and he went down on his face.

Instantly, Ed drew the chief's blade and held its point close to Jack's chest. Jack stopped.

'This happened a little sooner than I thought it would,' shrilled Ed. 'It makes no difference. George, tie his hands. Tappan, truss Chuckswilly up and put him in your wagon. Be sure to gag him, too.'

Jack said, 'What's going on?'

Ed's bloodied lips opened in a gap-toothed smile. 'Just a little scheme of mine, Cuz. We young bloods don't care for Chuckswilly's supercautious handling. We want action. Now. And I'm not going to allow anybody to stand between Polly and me.

'So I got twenty-five men, *real* men, to agree to attack your cadmen tonight. Chuckswilly thought they all went home, but they didn't. They're just hanging back.'

He was right. A minute later hoofs clattered. Ed greeted his friends and told them what had happened. Then he climbed into the front wagon, and the caravan started off at a fast pace.

Jack was put in the wagon. His legs and hands were tied, but he wasn't gagged. He shouted, 'Chuckswilly'll never forgive this. He'll kill you.'

'No, he won't. Why? Because while attacking the dog-eaters, our brave leader will die in the vanguard. He will become a martyr to the cause.'

Ed burst out laughing. In the middle of his laughter, a bright red-blue-and-white globe burst in the distant sky.

'That's Mowrey's rocket!' yelled Ed. 'Polly must be leaving the cadmus!'

Lashes drew blood. The riding became a frenzy of shouts for more speed, of violent lurches and bumps as the wagons, rounding curves, skidded off the road, of wind rushing past his sweating face, and a steady but vain tugging and wrenching at the ropes around his wrists.

The race, which should have been eternally long, went fast. By the time he had rope-burned his wrists until they bled, had cursed until his dry mouth and rasping throat forced silence, the train had pulled into the Cage barnyard.

Ed jumped down and beat on the closed door of the barn. Zeb, one of the indentured servants, stuck his head out of the open door of the hayloft. His eyes widened, and he disappeared. A moment later, the big bar was drawn, and the door swung in. The wagons drove in, one after the other. Ed told Zeb to shut the door.

Jack, struggling to his knees, saw his father rise from a pile of furs in a dark corner. He had puffy eyes, and the red marks on one side of his face showed he had slept in one position.

Jack wondered about his mother and sisters. They were not supposed to know anything about what was going on. How could they sleep through all the snortings and *whee-ha*ings of the unicorns, the grind of wooden axles, the beating on the door, the shouting? And his mother? She'd know Walt was staying all night in the barn. What excuse could he give to fool her?

In some ways, thought Jack, this was a most amateurish and unsecret plot. Not that that would matter if his cousin succeeded.

There was a rapping on the big door. Zeb swung open the small door within the larger. Josh Mowrey stepped through. He was pale beneath his dark skin, and his mouth worked.

'You see my rocket?'

'Yes,' said Ed. 'What does it mean?'

'I see Kliz, you know, the Catcher of the Larks, come down the highway from the direction of the mountains. He been gone for two weeks, you know.'

Josh paused for the confimation he so desperately seemed to need. Ed nodded.

'He goes into a cadmus, the second from the left as you face the creek, you know. Then, about an hour ago, he comes out with R'li and Polly O'Brien. They build a fire and sit around it for a while, talking and barbecuing ribs. They got a couple of big sacks, the kind you take on long trips. I watch. Nothing happens. But I get to thinking. If Polly's showing herself like that, it means only one thing. You know?'

Suddenly he began wheezing heavily and coughing. When he'd mastered his fits, he said, 'Damn it, Ed, can't we talk outside? You know I can't be near a unicorn without getting this asthma.'

'So what if everybody in Slashlark does know what's going on? Stay here. And cut out the details. You're not writing a book.'

Josh looked hurt.

'Well, if I get to wheezing, I'll be no good as a fighting man. Anyway, to me it meant she's getting ready for the Thrruk. But what's she waiting for? I can't tell; I'm too far away to hear them. And I don't care to crawl closer. You know how those horstels are, Ed. They can smell you a mile off and hear the drop of an eyelid. Isn't that so?'

Ed snarled, 'Drag this out any more and I'll stick you, so help me!'

Josh wheezed and said, 'Damn beasts! Don't get mad. Well, I'd just decided to sneak over, anyway, because I am a good stalker, you know. Then I saw something coming through the woods. When it was close enough so I could make out its outlines, my hair stood on end. That's not just a figure of speech, Ed. It *stood*. And was I happy I'd stayed where I was! I about filled my britches. You should have seen it.'

Wang's voice was getting shriller. 'Seen what?'

'Big as a house. Teeth three times as long as a bear's. A tail that could knock down a tree. Even though I didn't believe . . .'

'Do you want to die?'

'It was a dragon!'

Josh glanced about to soak up the astonishment and fear he had created.

Wang seemed to sense that if he didn't do something at once, he'd lose his command.

He shouted, 'All right! Dragon or not, we're attacking! Men, unload this equipment! If you're not sure how the weapons operate, read the instructions! Shake it! It's not too long until dawn!'

Jack became aware of two things at once. Chuckswilly had regained consciousness and was being helped down from Tappan's wagon. And his father was walking toward him, ignoring everyone's greetings, his eyes steady on his son but glazed. He held the scimitar in his left hand. His eyes were red and swollen with tears, and his beard was soaked.

'Son,' Walt spoke in a voice so low, so out of character, that Jack was frightened, 'Tony told your mother and me a thing he could no longer keep to himself.'

'And that was . . . ?'

'He saw you kissing that – that siren, R'li. Caressing her.'

'Well?'

Walt's voice remained subdued. 'You admit it?'

Jack refused to lower his eyes before his father's. 'Why not? I'm not ashamed of it.'

Walt gave a roar. He raised the scimitar. Ed grabbed his arm and wrenched so strongly that the blade fell to the ground. Walt gasped with pain and held his wrist, but he did not offer to pick up the weapon. Ed, however, stooped quickly to seize it.

As Walt stood there, breathing heavily, his eyes appeared to focus for the first time, to grasp that his son and his leader were both tied.

'Chuckswilly! What's going on?'

The dark man, ghastly with dried blood caking the side of his face, explained.

Walt could not move. Events were happening too fast for him. Struck from two sides, he could not decide which way to hit out. As a result, he did neither.

'We're raiding your cadmen tonight,' Ed told him. 'Are you helping us?' He swung the scimitar meaningfully.

'It's a revolt, is it?' whispered Walt. 'What'd Jack do? Stand up for Chuckswilly?'

'Oh, Jack's all right,' said Ed cheerily. The magic of the iron in his hand had uplifted him. 'Jack just lost his head for a minute. But he's thinking straight now. Aren't you, Cuz?

'The testimony about his making love to a siren would be

enough to condemn him to death on the spot. But, after all, he was just having a bit of fun. Weren't you, Jack? And sirens *are* beautiful. Not that Bess Merrimoth would appreciate hearing that. But she won't, will she, Jack? Why? Because you're going to kill off who first? Guess who?'

Jack said slowly, 'R'li.'

Ed nodded.

'That's the only way you'll redeem yourself. Wipe out your sin, and get in my good graces again, not to mention the Church's. Let me remind you that, from now on, it's going to be the correct thing in this county to be in my good graces.'

The ropes of the two bound men were cut. Even though Chuckswilly was now their prisoner, he was not handled roughly.

One of the men unloading the wagon said, 'Ed, what'll we do? All those guns and stuff, and nobody knows how to handle them.'

'Of course not,' Chuckswilly said scornfully. 'You bloody bucketing blowbrains never stopped to think you're going to need a lot of training before you become deadly with those. Why do you think I insisted this raid be cancelled? What good is a gun to you if you can't load it properly, let alone aim it? Who knows how to handle that glass cannon? And the flamethrowers? Lamebrained clodhoppers, you've failed before you started!'

'The hell we have!' blazed Ed. 'Men, if you've read the instructions, load your arms.'

He detailed a gang as cannoneers and another to pull the machine along on its wheels. Within an hour, he had rehearsed his men.

'Don't fire until you're so close you can't miss. They'll be paralyzed just from the noise.'

'And so will your men, the first time they pull the triggers,' muttered Chuckswilly.

Shortly after, the entire group marched down the highway. Chuckswilly and Jack Cage were in the lead. Both were armed with rapiers, but each had a man with a pistol pointed at him a few yards behind.

Ed had been given courage and an exaltation by the touch of the fabulous steel. He sang softly and coaxed his men until they came to a little path that ran from the road and into the woods. This led to Cadmus Meadow. The plan was to proceed upon it, dragging the cannon after them, until they burst out upon the field.

In the woods, the cannon's wheels sank into the soft mud. The whole company together could not get it going.

Ed swore and said, 'Abandon it. We don't need it, anyway.'

Subdued by the loss, nervous about what was ahead and their unfamiliarity with the firearms, the HKers walked on. Whenever a weapon clanked or a man cracked a twig, the rest shushed him.

At last they had only a few bushes between them and the field's broad sweep. There was the remnant of a fire glowing before one of the cadmus entrances, but no horstel was in sight.

'Flamethrowers to the front,' said Ed. His voice was strained, and he turned angrily to reprimand Josh for wheezing so loudly.

'There are twelve cadmi. When I give the signal, shoot your fire down the holes of the outer eight. Two men will stand guard at each of the other two entrances there. They will cut down anybody who tries to climb out. The remainder of the party will split into the designated halves. My men will follow me into the hole of the right-hand cadmus. The other half will follow Josh into the left. Chuckswilly will precede me; Jack will go before Josh. Walt, who do you want to go with?'

The elder Cage's eyes bulged. He shook his head and said hoarsely, 'I don't know. Wherever you want me.'

'Go with your son, then. Maybe you can keep him from turning coat and siding with the horstels.'

The Walt whom Jack knew would have knocked Ed down at that insult. This one shook his head and said, 'Boys, it isn't necessary to burn up all those goods stored underground. There's plenty for everybody to take home and enough left over for me. After all, it's my property. Don't wantonly destroy it. It isn't human to do so.'

Jack cried, 'Dad, for God's sake! Even at a time like this? What about the blood . . . ?'

Ed's fist silenced him. He staggered back, a salty wetness in his mouth.

Walt blinked as if he couldn't understand his son. 'Now that you've done . . . what you did, what else is there to think about?'

Then, in the next second, they had started to advance stealthily across the meadow.

The moon was bright with fullness. There was no wind. The

only sound was the rustle of shoes through the ruggrass, a muffled cough that several swore at under their breaths, the wheezing of Josh Mowrey.

The circles at the bases of the cadmi were black and seemingly empty. Jack could not help visualizing eyes staring out from the shadows and hands gripping bows and spears. Was an arrow even then being centred on his unarmored chest?

Ed whispered to Mowrey, 'Where do you suppose Polly is? Could she have left before we got here?'

Josh's eyes rolled whitely, and he wheezed, 'I don't know. I'm not worried about her. What I'd like to know is where's that dragon?'

Ed snorted and said, 'The only dragon you saw came from a bottle.'

'Not me! When I drink, I don't wheeze. And you can hear me now, can't you? But where in hell could it be?'

As if he had been overheard and was being answered, a bellow came from directly behind them. It was a roar such as none had ever heard, a throatiness and a basso profundo that made a bear's seem reedy.

They whirled; they screamed.

The thing rushing from the woods loomed twice as high as a tall man. It ran on two thick legs, its columnar body upright. The legs were crooked like a dog's hind limbs except for the feet, which spread five tremendous toes to support its weight. Two arms stretched straight out. Compared with the lower extremities, they looked tiny. Actually, they were thick as a man's body. Each of its three-fingered hands held a club, a young tree trunk.

The teeth flashed wickedly in the moonlight.

Its face was a mixture of beast and man: a high crest of cartilage on the bald pate, a tall forehead, thick supraorbital ridges, flaring lyre-shaped ears, a sloping canine muzzle, a heavy hominoid jaw, a prominent chin, and a bagging wrinkled reddish wattle. A dozen pencil-thick whiskers bristled from the sides of the grinning lips.

Even as it charged with a sound that rolled back from the surrounding forest like thunder from clouds, another bellow came from the creekbank. The men wheeled to see a second dragon.

Ed, screaming like a maddened unicorn, managed to make himself heard by some of his men. 'Flamethrowers! Shoot at them with your projectors! Fire'll scare them off!'

But the men were unfamiliar with their apparatus. Fright did not help their fumbling fingers. And half the twelve carrying the equipment threw it off their backs and ran.

One managed to ignite his thrower. A long fountain of red shot up into the night and fell, not on the oncoming monster, but on a group of men. Frantically, the thrower swerved his spray from them and toward the dragon. It was too late for half a dozen. Screaming, batting at their clothes, writhing on the ground, they burned. One ran for the creek. Halfway there, he fell and did not rise.

The flames forced the beast to pause, to whirl, to run around the mob in the hope it could get behind them where the projector could not reach it without frying other men.

Ed yelled, 'Shoot your guns at their bellies! They're soft!'

He raised his double-barreled flintlock pistol and pulled on both triggers.

The explosion stopped both monsters. They glared, looking here and there. However, neither seemed to be hit. No blood spurted from their white abdomens.

Some of the men took heart. They, too, raised their pistols and longbarrels and squeezed the triggers. Four or five misfired. A dozen barked.

A man fell, struck in the back by a comrade who had shot wildly.

The men reloaded. Fear made their motions frenzied and clumsy; they spilled the powder and dropped the bullets.

Silently the dragons charged. They were too close to be stopped, and the flamethrower could not hose them without searing the men. Moreover, one of the beasts threw a club over the heads of the crowd. It struck the flame handler in the chest and knocked him, unconscious or dead, to the ground.

The unattended projector emptied itself across the meadow.

A colossus stormed by Jack, its thick, tapering tail lashing from side to side. He threw himself to the ground in time to hear the *whish* of plated flesh as it just missed crushing his skull. He heard the thwack of it shattering the bones of the man behind him.

For a few seconds he lay hugging the ground, shaking uncontrollably. When he had mastered himself enough to raise his head, he saw that the man who had been struck was his father. He was on his back, and his mouth bubbled blood. His right arm was bent just below the elbow at a grotesque angle.

Jack had no chance to see more, for a huge body rushed at him. Once more, he clutched the meadow to his chest while both he and the ground shook. A five-toed, sharp-clawed foot as long as his arm crashed hard by his head. It lifted, seemingly into the sky, and he saw it no more.

But he did not leap up, for close behind the first dragon came the other, gripping George How between its teeth. George screamed and writhed. The jaws clamped down. The fat youth, like a distended sausage breaking at both ends from pressure in the middle, squirted blood from head and feet.

He gave one piercing shriek, 'Father!'

Then he dangled limply.

The first dragon turned its head and spoke. It sounded as if it said, in horstel child-talk, 'Some fun, heh, sister?'

The second did not reply. It bit through George's body, and the severed portions fell to the ground, close to Jack. George's nose was only a few inches from Jack's. The dead man's eyes were open in a gaze that seemed to Jack to say, 'You are next.'

Jack jumped up and ran. He did not aim for any particular destination, or he would not have fled to the nearest cadmus.

Just inside the entrance, he dived headlong. He didn't know whether the floor was six inches or sixty feet down. It seemed a hundred, but the bare earth floor was actually on a level with the meadow outside. Then and only then did he dare pause in his flight, to look back.

Others had the same idea. They were racing toward his shelter. Ed was in the lead, his short legs pumping desperately and his arm extended, with the scimitar held out at a forty-five degree angle from his body.

Just before Ed and the men behind him ran into the cadmus, another man arose belatedly from the seeming dead and tried to make the same flight. Even halfway across the meadow, the wheeze of Josh Mowrey could be heard. The dragons had, for that moment, quit their bellowing, and none of the wounded were crying out. For perhaps thirty seconds, there was one of those freakish silences that occur during even the noisiest battles. It was broken only by Josh's desperate, grating breath.

One of the dragons charged. Its footsteps thundered; it became a brutish figure outlined against the moon, its shadow blotting out the running pygmy. A huge arm raised. The club in its hand was a sinister chord bisecting the bright circle in the sky. It hung there a second and then dropped. There was a loud crack.

The wheezing was cut off. Josh was thrown forward by his own momentum plus that given by the blow. He slid for a dozen feet on the bloody and slippery grass, slid on his chest, for he had no head.

Then Jack's vision was curtained as the crowd forced him back into the cadmus.

Jack was shaken and his head whirled, but he realized he had an advantage over the newcomers. They were silhouetted by the moonlight, and they could not see him. It was easy to strike Ed's wrist with his fist and knock the scimitar from his grasp.

Ed yelled and clutched for his attacker with his uninjured hand. His cousin stooped over and picked up the blade and merged with the darkness.

'Stand back!' Jack shouted. 'Or I'll cut you down!'

A spark jumped in the shadows. A roar and a flash. Something whistled so close to his ear it brushed the lobe. He threw himself down just in time to escape a volley of three more pistol balls. The men charged, fell over his prostrate body, and piled upon and around him.

Nobody knew where the enemy was. They struck at each other, shouted, felt around for him, and were rewarded by blows.

A moment later, light dispelled the chaos. A torch was thrust into the cadmus hole and showed them their surroundings. But they had no thought for Cage. The hand gripping the flaming brand was huge and three-fingered.

The walls of the place they crouched in were formed of some hard and woody-looking substance. There was no exit other than the hole through which they had entered. Whatever passage existed had been so cleverly closed that no line of demarcation showed. If the invaders wanted to go farther they would have to blast their way with bombs. While they remained in the cone, they couldn't do that. And while the dragon waited outside, the men must stay right there.

Impasse.

Four men carried firearms. Three were busy trying to reload. The other was out of powder.

It wasn't bravery but sheer desperation that made Jack charge the thing that held the light.

He ran full into the glare, stared eye to eye with the monster, saw that the left canine in its open mouth was black with rot – he remembered that later – and swung the blade. Its sharp edge cut through the thumb gripping one side of the torch; digit and brand fell together to the floor.

Jack stooped to pick it up. As he did so, a gush of blood from the wound spilled down his neck. A roar deafened him as the sound waves bounced back and forth in the narrow chamber. Then he had scooped it up, turned, and flung the still burning wood at the men.

Several things occurred at once. He noticed the dragon's thumb was still curled around the torch, its long heavy nail embedded within the wood. Behind him, the roar shifted into a curiously pathetic wail followed by a lament in child-talk, 'My thumb, manling! Give me back my thumb!'

He paid no attention to the dragon. He stared at the wall behind the men, for it was opening. A man-high iris was splitting the brown glossy substance.

He cast aside his plan to try to dodge by the beast and to make a run for the woods. Instead, he swerved past the group and plunged into the fresh hole. He hoped that the time gained when the raiders had thrown up their arms to protect their eyes from his thrown torch would be enough for a good head start.

It was.

His enraged pursuers shouted. A pistol went off. He turned a corner and found himself in a narrow corridor. The sounds behind were cut off as if a door had closed.

A moment later he realized that that was exactly what had happened. For the entire hall, like a cyclopean hand, closed round him, pressed against his body, and squeezed so hard he thought his ribs would break and his blood would burst from his mouth and ears. But it was not that terrible pressure that forced consciousness from him. It was a tongue of flowing wallsubstance groping for all apertures; it shoved into his mouth and filled up his throat and cut off his breath. Thunder and darkness and panic seized him. And he knew no more.

Through a veil, light and sound.

R'li's voice.

'Is he dead?'

'Jack Cage?' said a male voice that Jack could not identify.

'No. His father.'

'He'll live. If he wants to.'

'O Speaker to the Soul, must you always be mouthing what you learned at the Rites?'

'It's true, isn't it?'

'But obvious and tiresome,' replied the siren. 'Walt Cage

will probably want to die when he finds out he's been dragged into a cadmus. He hates us so.'

'That's up to him.'

Jack opened his eyes. He was lying on a mound of some soft stuff in a large circular room. Its walls and floor were formed of the glossy brown flesh-vegetable. A twilight came from gray globular clusters that festooned both ceiling and walls. He sat up and touched the globes. He withdrew his fingers, but not because they were hot, for they were cool. The cluster had squirmed slightly.

He looked around. R'li and Polly O'Brien were watching the man across the room. His father was lying on a bed of the same mossy stuff that was under him.

Yath, the medicine man of the local Wiyr, was bending over Walt and adjusting bandages. Now and then he whispered into the man's ear. Why, Jack could not guess, because his father was gray with shock, unconscious.

Jack said, 'Yath, what's wrong with my father?'

Quickly R'li said, 'Please don't interrupt him, Jack. He shouldn't talk to anybody just now. But I'll tell you. Your father has three breaks in his right arm, two broken right ribs, and two compound fractures in his right leg, and possible internal bleeding. Naturally, he's in shock. We are doing all we can.'

Jack felt in his pockets. R'li held a smoke out to him and lit it while he sucked through it.

'Thanks. Now tell me, what the hell happened? The last I remember is that the walls were closing in on me.'

R'li smiled and picked up his hand. 'If we'd ever had time to talk about anything except ourselves, Jack, you'd have found out just what a cadmus is. I would have told you it's a living creature. Like the totumtree, it's half vegetable, half animal. Originally, it was a huge partly underground entity that lived in symbiosis with bears or mandrakes. Or, in fact, with anything that would provide it with meat or vegetation. In return for food, it offered shelter and protection from enemies. If, however, you failed to keep up the rent, you became an enemy and went into the empty belly sac.

'When I say it "offered" shelter, I didn't mean in any intelligent sense. It has no brain; not as we know it, anyway. But when we were building our new civilization, we bred these cadmi for larger size, for more "intelligence," for all the qualities we desired. The result is the creature you are now in.

One that provides you with fresh air, a constant and comfortable temperature, light, and safety. Actually, our underground dwelling is a colony of twelve such beasts, each of which grows the almost indestructible horn you see sticking from the meadow.'

'It's as simple as that? Why, then, the mystery all these centuries?'

'The information has always been available. But your leaders made it forbidden to you. They know the truth. But they prefer to allow the rank and file to regard cadmi as chambers of horror and evil magic.'

Jack ignored that. 'But how do you control it? How did it know we were enemies?'

'Before you can establish an "agreement" with a cadmus, you must offer it a certain amount of food at certain orifices. After that, it recognizes you by your odor and weight and shape. The walls of a room enfold you and take your shape-print.

'We teach it to react in such-and-such a manner to us, and from then on we're its masters – or partners – as long as the food comes in. But it's trained to sieze unidentified people and hold them until we order it to release them. Or to kill.'

She held out her hand to one of the light clusters. 'Look.'

As the hand neared, the globes brightened. When the hand withdrew, the light dimmed. Stroked three times, the cluster increased its brightness and retained it even after she took her fingers away.

'They'll hold that intensity until caressed twice. It's a matter of establishing communication and of training.'

Jack didn't know what he wanted to find out next. The attack, Ed, Polly, the dragons, his father, his present status.

He groaned.

R'li looked alarmed. He was glad of that because, in a way, it answered the question that had suddenly struck him. 'What did you think of me when you found me among the raiders?'

Leaning over, she kissed him full on the lips. 'I knew all about what was going on. We have our sources of information.'

'I should have stood up to them from the beginning. I should have told them to go to hell.'

'Yes, and ended up like poor Wuv,' she said.

'When did you find out about that?'

'Some time ago. Through certain – ah – channels.'

'Then you know all about the HK?'
'Yes.'
Yath, looking up, gestured.
She said, 'We're interfering with his work on your father.'
R'li led them into another cell. After Polly had stepped through, R'li stroked the iris three times, and it closed.
Jack would have liked to stay where they were, for a cadman was talking into a large metal box with needles and dials on its front. Once he stopped, and a male voice issued from the box. R'li beckoned them on; they went into another room where O'Reg, her father, was seated at a table.
The Blind King did not bother with greetings.
'Please sit down, Jack. I'd like to explain a few things about your immediate future. Especially since your fate concerns my daughter's.'
Jack wanted to ask just how much he knew about R'li and himself, but O-Reg evidently did not want to be interrupted.
'First, your father is going to be very much disturbed because he was brought into a cadmus without his permission. But it was either that or allow him to die while waiting for a human doctor.
'He'll have to wait until he's much better before he can make a decision. But it's vital that Polly and you decide at once what you want to do. We've received word that news of this attack has reached Slashlark and that the entire garrison is now marching out to surround the farm.
'Ten minutes ago, their vanguard, riding on carriages, dashed past the Watcher of Squamous Creek. Foot soldiers are following. That means that the wheelmen will be here in about an hour and a half.
'Their ostensible purpose is to safeguard us Wiyr from an aroused citizenry. Actually, they may be looking for an excuse to invade our cadmi. They know we've captured HKers. They may reason that we've extracted their secrets and that it'd be best to launch the attack against the horstels ahead of schedule.
'However, let's hope they wouldn't dare do so without word from the capital. It's day now; the Government heliographs have been very busy. Inasmuch as it's fifteen hundred miles from here to St. Dyonis, it'll be some time before Slashlark gets a message.
'But the soldiers will soon be here. They are as excited as the citizens about the affair; there's no telling what'll happen

if discipline is forgotten. So, in case they should violate sanctuary, you'd better decide now what you want to do.

'You've two choices. One, take your chance in court. Two, flee into the Thrruk.'

'You don't leave much choice,' said Jack. 'The first is certain death in the mines.'

Despite his concentration on the Blind King, he noticed that Polly O'Brien had been edging up to him. Her huge eyes were half-lidded; one hand was held behind her long skirt as if she were hiding something in it. Jack's first thought was that she had a knife. It was easy for him to think so. Too many people had been out to get him these last few hours. His second thought was that she had no reason to stick him in the ribs and that he was getting oversensitive, too nervous.

A cadman stepped into the chamber and spoke in adult-talk to O-Reg. O-Reg said in English, 'I'll be back in a moment.'

After he left, Jack said, 'Does my father have much chance to pull out of this?'

'I can't guarantee anything,' R'li replied in child-talk. 'But Yath is very capable. He has his ear to the Great Mother's bosom. He's one of the best of the healer class.'

At another time, Jack would have been both surprised and made curious by this remark. He had not suspected that the Wiyr had classes of any sort. Professions and trades, yes, but the word she had used could not be translated into English to mean either of those terms. It had an enclitic particle – the *pang* which signified that the noun it modified had qualities that were definitely bounded by certain restrictions. Thus, in certain contexts, it could indicate that the restricted person designated by the noun had been born into the situation and could not get beyond these limits.

If anybody had asked him before this particular conversation, Jack would have replied that he had only a vague idea of how cadmus society was arranged. If pressed, he would have said that he had always thought of the Wiyr as living in near anarchy.

But, right now, he could think only of his father.

R'li continued, 'Yath has already repaired the broken bones. Aside from shock, for which your father has been treated, and possible internal bleeding, Walt should be able to get up and walk now.'

Polly O'Brien gasped, and she said, 'Black magic!'

'No,' R'li replied. 'Knowledge of Nature. Yath set the

bones and then injected a very powerful and quick-drying glue that binds the broken bones together more strongly than they were before the breaks. He has also administered several drugs, the combined effect of which combats shock. And he has placed you father in a *kipum*. Translated roughly, a *kipum* is a trance in which the patient is wide open to psychic suggestions that enable the body to heal itself more swiftly and efficiently.

'No, there is no sorcery or witchcraft about our methods. If Yath would explain his methods, the techniques of his profession, the ingredients and formulas of his medicines, you would clearly see that no magic is involved. But he won't tell you any more than he would me. His powers are the secrets of his profession, That is one of the privileges of his class. He may never be a king, but he has rights that must be respected.'

O-Reg came back into the room. He said, 'Chuckswilly escaped Mar-Kuk and Hya-Nun, the dragons. He's contacted the unicorn soldiers and is now on his way here with them. We'll know in a few minutes what he wants.'

He paused, then resumed, 'I expected that he'll demand that we surrender you, Jack. In fact, he'll want every human being now in this cadmus. That means Polly, your father, Ed Wang, and his fellows.'

R'li, her face anxious, stared up at Jack. 'Don't you see what this means? All of you, no matter what your motives for entering here, will be condemned. You know your law! If you go into a cadmus, you are guilty by contamination. You'll be automatically convicted and sentenced. The only doubt will be whether you burn at the stake or work in the mines!'

'I know that,' Jack said. He grinned lopsidedly. 'In a way, it's funny about Ed. His hatred for you horstels and those humans who associate with them has hurled him headlong among them. And now, like it or not, he must share their fate.'

O-Reg said, 'Ed Wang doesn't think it's so funny. I told him what's facing him, and he almost fainted with anger and frustration. Also, I believe, with more than a little fear. I left him howling obscenities and threats.'

O-Reg made a face of disgust. 'A vile creature!'

'What are you going to do?' R'li said to Jack.

'If I stay here, what will happen? Not that I want to stay. I couldn't remain below the ground for ever.'

'Nor would we like to be shut up within our homes,' O-Reg said. 'You know how much we love the open skies, the trees, our fields. Although we are accustomed to descend into the cadmi for protection and for necessary business, we, too, would go mad if forced to be contained for long periods in these cells.

'However, that possibility need not be our concern at the moment. I'll tell you what's happening outside these walls. As you guessed, the government of Dyonisa has been preparing to attack the horstels within its boundaries. Moreover, Dyonisa is in league with Croatania and Farfrom. All three governments plan to exterminate us Wiyr, kill every one, man, woman, child.

'We've known this for some time. But, so far, we've not known what to do. We were prepared to give up much to preserve the peace, but we would not surrender our independence and way of life. However, the human governments do not want mediation and adjustment. They want to solve the problem completely, forever, and at once. So . . . '

Jack said, 'If you know you have to fight, why don't you strike first? Be realistic.'

'We have made preparations,' R'li said. 'We will use all the forces of Baibai, our Mother.'

She referred to a deity or a force, Jack was not certain which. He suspected that Baibai was an earth goddess, a false deity, a demon to be abhorred by all Christians. It was said that the horstels sacrificed their children to her, but Jack did not believe that. No one who knew the horstels and their revulsion against the shedding of blood, the protective rituals with which they surrounded themselves even in the slaughter of food animals, could believe that. Nevertheless, there were other evils besides child-sacrifice.

O-Reg smiled grimly and said, 'The HK Society was not an official organization, but I'm sure that the government knew of its existence and even planted agents among it to encourage its plans. However, I have news for you.

'The capital city of Dyonisa is on fire.'

'It's what?' said Jack.

'It's burning. A fire broke out in the slums. Fanned by a strong wind, it spread throughout the wooden tenement districts. Moreover, it's threatening the houses of the merchants and nobility. The refugees from the slums of Dyonisa are streaming out through the gates of the city walls and into the countryside. I suspect that the government will have other things on its mind and on its hands than war against the Wiyr. At the moment, anyway.'

'Who started the fire?' asked Polly O'Brien.

O-Reg shrugged and said, 'What's the difference? The slums have been a tinderbox, a firetrap, for a long time. This was bound to happen. But you can be sure that, whatever the cause, the horstels will be blamed.'

Jack wondered how O-Reg knew so swiftly what was happening in the capital, so far away. Then he remembered the talkboxes. But 1,200 miles away!

'A few more minutes,' O-Reg said, 'and you will have to stay here. Your passage out will be blocked by the soldiers.'

A horstel male entered and spoke to O-Reg in adult-talk. The Blind King answered; the messenger left. O-Reg switched to English.

'Ed Wang and his companions have left. They ran for the woods, toward the Thrruk, I suppose.'

R'li placed her hand on Jack's shoulder and said,' You can't surrender to them! If you do, you'll be executing yourself. You'll die!'

'But what about my father?' Jack said.

She replied, 'He'll probably get well, and soon. But he'll have to spend at least a day in bed.'

'I won't desert him!' Jack said. He clamped his jaws firmly and glared at the others.

O-Reg said, 'What about you, Polly O'Brien?'

Her heart-shaped face with the enormous eyes had lost its beauty. She was very pale; the skin around the eyes was stained a deep blue; the eyes were very restless. She looked at Jack, then at the horstels.

'You make up your mind what you want to do,' Jack said. 'I'm going to see my father.'

He walked out of the cell and down the long oval corridor, barely wide enough for two people to pass each other. The walls were greenish-gray, smooth, without grain, and shiny. Every few feet, clusters of the globes hung from fleshy-looking stalks attached to the ceiling. Most of these were illuminated. But the light was that of twilight, and there was no sound except that of his feet on the slightly springy and somewhat cold floor. On each side, about every twenty feet, was a slit, the mark of a closed iris.

Once, on his right, he passed a half-opened iris, and he

looked within. The cell just beyond was a very large one and much brighter than any he had seen. The walls were a dull orange streaked with jagged light green. In the middle of the floor, covered with rugs made of unicorn and tailbear hides and several unidentifiable skins, was a wide, very low, round table of a light-brown and shiny wood. Around it were piled more furs, apparently for those who wished to sit or lie down on them.

Against the wall opposite him was an iris fully open, and through this he got a glimpse of a female, about five years old, looking up at a siren. Presumably, the siren was the child's mother. Then the siren looked up from the child and saw Jack Cage. Her reaction was not at all what he would have expected. Surprise, embarrassment, a slight consternation, yes. But not the horror on her face. Even at that distance he could see her go pale, and the suddenly open mouth indicated a gasp.

He did not wait to see more but walked on. Yet he could not help considering that what she revealed in a moment of shock might be what she and most of her kind really felt about the human beings. Usually they were amiable or, at the least, polite in their dealings with men. Under that easy exterior, did they hide feelings toward man similar to man's toward them?

A moment later, he entered the cell where his father lay. Yath was still crouched by the side of Walt Cage and whispering into his ear. But now, even though Walt was unconscious or in a deep sleep, his skin was ruddy or pink. Moreover, there was a slight smile on his lips.

Yath stopped whispering and rose. 'He will sleep for some time, then he will be ready to eat and to walk about a little.'

'How soon can he walk out of here?'

'In about ten hours.'

'How strong will he be then?'

Yath shrugged and said, 'Depends on the man. Your father is very strong. I think he will be able to walk several miles – at a slow pace. If you are thinking of taking him with you to the Thrruk very soon, do not. It will be several days before he could stand the rigors of flight through that wilderness.'

'I wish I could talk to him,' Jack said.

'You will have to wait a while,' Yath replied. 'By then, the meadows above us and the woods around will be infested with soldiers. No, my boy, you cannot get him to tell you what to do. You must make a choice for yourself and soon.'

A voice came through the iris from the corridor outside. 'Jack!'

Recognizing Polly, Jack left the room. She thrust a roughly cylindrical object, wrapped in a white cloth and bloody at one end, at him.

'The dragon's thumb,' she said. 'R'li was going to throw it away, but I took it. She laughed at me, even though I was keeping it for you.'

'Why?'

'Brainless! Didn't you know that Mar-Kuk almost tore up the horn of this cadmus trying to get her thumb back? She failed, but she swore she'd kill you if she ever saw you again, and she'd get her precious thumb. I don't know how, but she knew your name. Probably the horstels told her some time ago, while she was robbing our farms. Anyway, she said that the next time she saw you, she'd mangle you. Which she will, unless you . . . '

'Unless I what?'

'Unless you have this, a part of her body. I know. My mother was a chemist, remember? And she did know more of horstel lore than she should have. She dealt in dragon bones, those dug up by miners or found by hunters. They bring a high price because they're supposed to make a wonderful heart medicine if ground up and drunk in wine. Also, an aphrodisiac.

'My mother told me some things about the dragons. They are very superstitious. They believe that if another person gets hold of a part of their body, a tooth, a claw, anything, that person can control them. Of course, Mar-Kuk is banking on your not knowing that, but she wants to kill you before you find out. Moreover, a dragon believes that if she dies with any part of her body missing, she's doomed to wail through their hell as a misshapen ghost.'

Jack looked at the thumb, then put it in his jacket pocket. 'Why would I need it unless I intended to leave the cadmus right now?' he said. 'Did you think I was going to do that?'

'Of course! We both had better get out as quickly as we can and run like hell! The soldiers will start digging us out, you can bet your soul on that! They'll kill everybody. We'd be trapped!'

'I'm not going,' he said. 'I can't desert my father.'

'Or leave that siren behind! Could you really be in love

with *her?* Or is what they say about sirens true? The things they do to make a man fall into their spells?'

Jack flushed and said, 'She'd go with me if I asked her. Or even without my asking her. No, I don't want to desert my father.'

'Then you'll make a useless gesture. You'll be sacrificing yourself and your father both! I'm getting out!'

A tall red-haired satyr was approaching them. He carried a small leather bag.

'We'd better go now,' he said to Polly. 'The soldiers are almost here.'

Polly said to Jack, 'It's not too late to change your mind. Siyfiy will guide us through the mountains.'

Jack shook his head. Polly said, 'You're a fool!'

Jack watched the two walk swiftly away until the upward curve of the hall took them out of sight. Then he re-entered the room where his father lay. A few minutes later, R'li and her father came in.

'The soldiers have just surrounded the cadmuses,' O-Reg said. 'Captain Gomes and Chuckswilly have demanded that we surrender all human beings. I am going out now to talk to them.'

He embraced and kissed R'li and then walked out. Jack said, 'You two act as if you thought you might never see each other again.'

'We always kiss each other, even if we've going to be parted for just a few minutes. Who knows? At any time, we may be parted forever in this world. But, in this case, there *is* great danger.'

'Perhaps my father and I should give ourselves up,' Jack said. 'There is no compelling reason why your whole group should be in peril.'

R'li looked impatient. 'Please don't talk that way any more. It's not as if we had a choice. Those *tarrta* [a horstel word for the terrestrials meaning *latecomers*] want to attack us as much as they do you.'

Jack paced back and forth. R'li sat down on a pile of furs and began to hum and to comb her hair with her *pekita*. Her absolute self-control and relaxed appearance irritated him. Savagely he said, 'Are you people really *human?* How can you be so calm?'

She smiled and said, 'Because it's needful. What good would it do for me to waste myself in the evil of worry and fretting?

If I could do something positive, I'd be doing it. But I can't. So I send my concerns to a small corner of my mind. I know they're there, but they're veiled.'

Uncomprehendingly, he stared at her.

She said, 'If you had ever been through the Rites, darling, you'd be able to do the same thing. And you'd be very happy you had the ability.'

A female horstel entered. She said, 'Jack Cage, O-Reg wants you to show yourself to Gomes and Chuckswilly. They are claiming that you've been murdered. They threaten to invade us unless they can see you. O-Reg says that you do not have to come if you do not wish to.'

'They know Polly O'Brien was here,' Jack said. 'What about her?'

'She is out there, too. The soldiers came too swiftly; she couldn't get away in time.'

R'li arose and said, 'I'll go out with you, Jack.'

'I don't think you should. This demand may just be a way for them to grab Polly and me. Maybe they're planning to kill the horstels above ground, too. No, you better stay here.'

'I'm coming with you. Don't argue, please.'

As they walked through the corridors, Jack said to the female who had brought the message. 'What did they say about my father?'

'Gomes wanted to see him, too. O-Reg explained that he was hurt too badly to come. But Gomes said that he would take your word for it that your father is safe.'

'I scent a trap,' Jack said. 'Why are they so concerned about us? We've taken sanctuary and so put ourselves beyond the law of Dyonisa. What do they care what happens to us?'

'I doubt if they do,' R'li replied. 'But they're looking for any excuse at all to attack us. We're trying to placate them as much as possible.'

The other siren said, 'We won't be entirely helpless if they do try to seize the *tarrta* or attack us. O-Reg has fifty armed warriors with him. We are showing them that we won't be taken like a puppy.'

They stepped through the iris into the chamber within the horn of the cadmus and then out onto the meadow. The sun had been up for about an hour, and the meadow was bright. Near the cadmus entrance stood O-Reg and a group of satyrs with bows and arrows and spears. Polly O'Brien was a few paces behind the Blind King.

Two men were talking to O-Reg. Gomes, the captain of the garrison, was a short, stocky man with a broad face and a thick, yellow mustache. He wore the conical, leather-covered helmet, leather cuirass, and long kilt of the Dyonisan soldier. His broad leather belt supported a scabbard and a holster for a flintlock pistol with a glass barrel. The glass rapier, however, was in his hand. Chuckswilly stood by him. Behind the two, at a distance of forty yards, were several hundred soldiers and about fifty armed civilians. These were arranged in a crescent, the horns of which curved inward toward the cadmus. Most of them were archers or spearmen, but a small group bore flintlock glass muskets.

Gomes, seeing Jack Cage, called out, 'Are you being kept there against your will? Is your father alive?'

Jack Cage opened his mouth to speak boldly but found the words were caught in his throat. For the first time, with the eyes of so many human beings on him, most of whom represented the authority of his country, he realized fully what he was doing. He was a traitor. Worse, he had gone over to the enemies of mankind and to soulless beings who rejected his God. He would be excommunicated, damned forever, he would burn for eternity. His name would be a curse word; every man would despise and hate him.

R'li, who was standing behind him, touched his shoulder. 'I know how you must feel,' she whispered. 'No man could lightly cut himself off from his own. If you can't do it, I'll understand.'

Later, he found himself wondering if she had known just what to do to precipitate him over the cliff. Was she so good a psychologist that she understood exactly what nerve to stimulate in him, precisely what components of his pride and his love for her to trigger?

At that moment, he did not think at all or was not conscious of taking any thought. He turned, placed his arm around her waist, and swung around to face Gomes and Chuckswilly. Then he kissed R'li full and hard on the lips.

A shout broke from the soldiers and the civilians. Gomes cried, 'You filthy whoreson!'

O-Reg looked startled. He moved close to Jack and said fiercely. 'You fool! Are you trying to start a battle here? Do you want us to be killed?'

He stepped back and said, 'Well, the damage's done. There's no turning back for you now, Jack Cage. Nor for any of us.'

'I love you,' R'li said.

Jack was so overcome with what he had done and the suddeness of it that he was faint. His heart, which had been beating hard enough before, now hammered at his breast.

O-Reg's voice roared above the others. 'You have your answer! Jack Cage has voluntarily entered and wishes to remain with us. As for his father, he will be released as soon as he is able to walk – if he wants to return to you.'

Chuckswilly shouted, 'You have used your satan's magic to pervert that poor boy's soul! I cannot believe that he would do this if he were in full possession of his faculties! I demand that you hand him over so that our doctors and priests may examine him!'

O-Reg smiled savagely. 'And if you find that he is in his right mind, you will then let him come back to us? Do we have your promise to do that?'

'Of course you do. I will swear on the Bible that he will be set free,' Chuckswilly said.

'Our fathers had some experience with your fathers and their Bible-swearing when you people first came here,' O-Reg said. 'We saw how much you value the resentment of your deity against oath-breakers. No, thank you.'

Gomes was rigid as a statue except for his right hand, which tugged at the whiskers on the edge of his moustache. Obviously he was trying to make a decision.

But Chuckswilly did not wait for him to speak. He turned to face the soldiers, and he bellowed, 'Seize the heretics and sorcerers!'

Some soldiers stepped forward, then halted when they saw the uncertainty of the others. Gomes came out of his rigidity and shouted, 'I'm in command here! Back to your posts!'

Jack said to O-Reg, 'There's nothing to be gained by talking any more. I think we should return to the cadmus! And fast!'

'You're right,' O-Reg said. 'You and Polly O'Brien go first. We'll cover you. R'li, you go with Jack.'

'No, you don't!' Chuckswilly cried. He drew his rapier and ran at Jack. O-Reg stepped in front of him and lifted the Blind King's staff to protect himself. The rapier drove in past the staff and entered O-Reg's solar plexus. He shrieked and fell backward with Chuckswilly on top of him.

Jack pushed R'li and yelled, 'You and Polly get out of here!'

Without waiting to see if they were obeying, he turned around again. O-Reg's staff was lying by his dead hand, and his killer was just getting to his feet. Jack jumped forward, stooped, picked up the staff, and brought it down hard against Chuckswilly's leather helmet. The man groaned and pitched, face down, on the corpse of the Blind King.

There was a whistle as an arrow flew past his ear. A horstel screamed behind Jack. Then the air was thick with feathered shafts. A few guns fired. Jack threw himself on the ground by the two bodies but leaped up a second later. One glance showed him that the fire of both sides had taken its toll. Polly and R'li were lying on the ground, but they were alive and unhit.

'Run for it!' he screamed at them. He picked up Chuckswilly's rapier and faced the horde running toward him across the meadow. The soldiers and civilians who had not been downed by the first volley had abandoned discipline and were trying to get to the horstels before they could shoot a second time. They did not make it. The horstels, acting under the barked commands of their officer, fired again.

Those in the forefront of the attackers crumpled. Those behind them leaped over their bodies and closed in on the archers.

Gomes parried the spear thrust of a horstel and backed away. Jack, yelling, ran up to him and drove the point of his rapier into the captain's neck. Gomes fell backward, taking the blade with him and tearing it out of Jack's hand. Jack stared at the open dead eyes of Gomes and the rapier projecting halfway from the neck. Then a soldier with a short stabbing spear was on him.

Jack wrenched the rapier from the flesh of Gomes and brought the blade up just in time to deflect the soldier's thrust. With the other hand, he seized the shaft of the spear and jerked the man to him. He brought the rapier around and slammed its round blade against the side of the man's neck. As the soldier fell forward, Jack brought his knee up against his chin. He leaped back; the soldier crumpled unconscious to the grass.

Afterward he did not remember much detail. It was mostly thrust and parry and jump and run. He did not think he wounded or killed anybody after that. The second he got a chance, he retreated from the one attacking him. His first concern was R'li; therefore, he tried to get back to the cadmus entrance.

When he did so, he found the opening was half blocked by fallen bodies and fully blocked by a meelee of men and horstels. Then he saw R'li and Polly O'Brien running away from the cadmus. There was a space of about twenty yards forming an avenue to the woods by the side of the meadow, and the two women were running down it. Jack yelled after them without thinking that they could not possibly hear him above the shouts, shrieks, din of weapons on weapons, and the occasional explosion of a firearm.

He ran after them. When he was halfway down the avenue, it closed up again. He had to fight and dodge his way from then on. Twice he was knocked down, and once he felt a sharp flint drive into his side. But he fell back; the point came out; the man holding the spear stepped forward to lunge again. But the soldier dropped the weapon and reached behind him to try to pull out the knife that had been stuck into him by a horstel.

Jack got away without thanking his savior and began to crawl. Strangely, or not so strangely, this method of escape proved the swiftest and safest. Those who saw him, if any did pay any attention, must have thought that he was too badly wounded to bother with.

R'li and Polly were hiding behind some bushes. He turned to look at the field. By now the human beings were running for their lives. Horstels had poured out of the other cadmus exits, and in a short time, overwhelmed the soldiers and civilians. They could have overtaken those running away, but for some reason they had chosen not to do so.

R'li was weeping. Jack tried to comfort her, but he could not stop her wailings. Polly said, 'Let her cry it out. Oh, my God!'

Jack looked at where she was pointing. He echoed her cry. Several hundred reinforcements, all armed with muskets, were trotting across the meadow.

The horstels, seeing them, began to pick up their dead and wounded. Before they could get them safely into the cadmuses, the soldiers had formed into two ranks each, strung across the meadow. An officer shouted commands. The first row sank to one knee and aimed their weapons.

'Fire!'

At least thirty hortels fell to the ground. The others, either panicking or knowing the futility of trying to rescue their casualties, ran to the entrances of the cadmi. At several of these, they had trouble all getting through at once. The second volley caught many of them.

Jack took R'li's hand and said, 'We can't get back in now. We're cut off. We'll have to run for the Thrruk.'

R'li did not move; she did not seem to hear him. He rotated her slowly so that she could not see the slaughter, and he pulled her away. Blindly, stumbling, tears coursing down her face and body, her face twisted, she allowed herself to be led away. Polly was gone, and he hoped that she was not so foolish as to think that she could get back into the graces of Dyonisa again.

Polly reappeared from behind a tree. In one hand she was holding a bow and a strap from which hung a quiver of arrows. In the other she had a bloody glass stiletto. Her eyes were huge. She looked strange.

'Where'd you get those?' he said.

'I knew we'd be as good as dead if we went into the Thrruk without weapons,' she said. 'I sneaked back and picked these up off the edge of the meadow. The bows and arrows, that is. The other, I took off a priest.'

'Took it?'

'After I stabbed him. The fat man of God was standing behind a tree and watching the slaughter. I suppose he meant to come out later, bless the survivors, and give the dead and dying the last rites. But I came up from behind him, snatched the knife from his belt, and stuck it in his big belly when he turned around to see who it was. The swine! He was one of those who tortured my mother until she died!'

Jack was shocked even while he was glad that Polly was not a weak and helpless woman. To get through the Thrruk, each one of their party would have to be tough and capable. R'li would be all right once she got over the first thrust of grief.

They walked swiftly as possible through the woods. Jack kept looking back, but he saw no men. By now, either the firing had stopped or the trees were cutting off the sound.

They came to a broad but shallow stream that fell down a series of small cataracts. The water was clear and very cold. They drank deeply and then washed off the dirt, sweat and blood. The wound in Jack's side had bled for a little while, then the blood had coagulated. Seeing it, R'li gave the first evidence of coming out of her bereavement. She looked through the plants along the side of the brook and presently came back with a heart-shaped flower with red and black petals.

After she cleaned Jack's wound, she placed the flower against the opening. 'Hold it there for about an hour. I will wash off the pieces that stick to the wound, and you should be all right after that.'

After kissing Jack lightly, she stood up and looked at the mountains in the distance to the north. They towered so high that they seemed near. All three knew, however, that the foot of the closest was at least three days' journey away.

'It's hot,' Polly said. She rose, unbuttoned the front of her long, billowing dress, and removed it. Underneath was not the thick underblouse and two thick petticoats he had expected. She wore nothing except the buskins on her feet.

'Don't look so shocked,' she said. 'You're not bothered if R'li goes naked.'

'But . . . but . . . you're human!'

'Only if you disregard the attitude of the Mother Church. She seems to think that witches are outside the pale of humanity.'

Jack was speechless from astonishment and also a fear.

Polly stood before him and turned around slowly until she made a complete circle. Even in his upset state, he noted that she had a beautiful and delightfully curved body.

She smiled at him and said, 'Did you think that my mother and I were innocents who were unjustly persecuted by the Church? No, our accuser was right, even if by accident. Riley told the priests that my mother was a witch because he wanted to have the only chemist shop in Slashlark. Unwittingly, he hit the mark.

'My mother is dead, and the day will soon come when Riley will die also. My coven would have killed him long ago, but I made them wait until I could slay him myself. It looks now as if I may have to wait a while. But when I do get my hands on him . . . '

She licked her lips, so full and pretty they looked as if they ought to be dedicated to nothing but kissing. She said, 'He'll take longer to die than even my mother did.'

R'li looked at Polly as if she were a poisonous and loathsome cyclops worm. Polly said, 'Not so hoity-toity, my kilt-pussied beauty. You should know how I feel; you've experienced enough humiliation and injury from the Christians.'

'So it's true,' Jack said slowly, 'that there were witches among the Earth people taken by the Arra?'

'True. But we don't worship the male demon you think we do. He's not the highest deity; he's the Great Goddess's son and lover. We worship the White Mother, She Whose religion is far, far older than that of you Johnny-come-lately Christians. Someday she will triumph. You don't know the truth about us. All you're heard are the lies and the distortions your fat priests give you.'

She rolled her clothes into a bundle. 'I'll just wear these when it gets colder or if we get in thorn bushes. It's wonderful not to have to wear clothes, to feel free again.'

'Is it true that you witches and warlocks have magical powers?' Jack said.

'We know some things you Christian don't,' Polly replied. She glanced at R'li and continued, 'But very few things that the Wiyr don't. They're as much witches as we. They worship the Great Mother, and . . . '

'But we don't sacrifice our babies to Her!' R'li said.

Polly started but recovered herself. She laughed. 'How did you know that? Do you have spies among us? Impossible! Some witch who must have been forced to go cadmus must have told you that. Well, what if we do? It doesn't happen very often, and the infant who is lucky enough to be slain in honor of Her is assured of an eternal and ecstatic life in the House of the Great Mother Herself.

'Besides, you're in no position to throw stones. It was only because of the presence of the Earthmen, becausc of their predictable reaction, that you Wiyr quit making human sacrifices to your Goddess. Now, confess, isn't that true?'

'No,' R'li said levelly. 'We outlawed that horrible rite at least fifty years before the Arra brought your ancestors to us.'

'This arguing will get us noplace,' Jack said. 'We need each other. R'li says that it's four hundred miles to the valley of the Thrruk. We have to climb some very high mountains, go through some very dangerous country. There are thrruks, mandrakes, werewolves, human outlaws, tailbears, and God only knows what else between us and our goal.'

'There are also Socinian patrols,' R'li said. 'They have become quite active these last few months.'

They picked up their weapons and began walking along the stream. R'li was at the head of their line because she knew where they would have to go. First, they must reach the Argulh Valley. From there on, she would be able to guide them with certainty. Until they got there, however, she would not have her bearings. All they had to do, she assured them, was to work their way upcountry. Eventually, they would come to a path that would take them to the Idoh. It was on the other side of the nearest peak, the Phul. This rose straight up for at least six thousand feet, then curved outward. It looked from this distance like a small-headed mushroom or a club.

'Around the other side is a broad and deep valley,' she said. 'When we get across that, we have to start climbing along the face of the Plel Massif. The Idoh Pass is at its farther end, high up.'

Jack stopped. 'I don't know, R'li. Maybe we should stay here awhile. I was all for running away at first because things looked so hopeless. But your cadmus might hold out. If it does, I might be able to get my father out of it some night. Then there are my brothers and sisters. What'll happen to them?'

R'li looked wonderingly at him. 'Jack,' she said softly, haven't you fully grasped what you did when you kissed me in front of all those humans? You *have* no family any more!'

'That doesn't mean I don't care about them.'

'I know. But they would have *nothing* to do with you. They might try to kill you the moment they saw you!'

'I'm hungry,' Polly said. 'Why don't you quit trying to mend things that are forever broken and think about our needs? If we don't fill our bellies and find a place to bed down for the night, we'll die. Soon.'

'All right. Give me the bow and quiver,' he said. 'I'll go hunting.'

'Nothing doing,' she said firmly. 'They're mine. I risked my life to get them; I'm keeping them.'

Jack became angry. 'We have to have a captain if we're going to get through this alive! I'm the man here! I should have the weapons and the say-so!'

'You haven't proved you're the man here,' Polly said. 'Besides, I'll bet anything that I'm the better hunter! You don't know me well.'

'She's right about the hunter part,' R'li said. 'I've seen her in the forest before.'

Polly gave the siren a curious look, but she smiled. Jack shrugged, unclenched his fists, and began looking along the bank of the stream. Polly disappeared into the woods. Presently he found several flints that had been washed down from the mountain. After ruining several, he shaped a serviceable knife. He searched for and found a totumtree with a branch of the proper thickness. Using the knife, he hacked off the branch. After whittling off the twigs and roughness along its length, he sharpened its end. By then his knife needed reworking, but he had a spear.

'I'll fire-harden its point tonight,' he said to R'li. 'Find some stones suitable for throwing. If I can kill an animal with them, I'll use its skin to make a sling.'

The two hunted through the woods for three hours. During that time, they saw only a barefox. Jack caught it in the ribs with a stone and rolled it over. But the hairless rodent jumped up at once and, yipping, fled into the underbush. By then it was time to return to meet Polly beneath a kingtree.

Polly was waiting for them. She was already busy degutting and skinning a wild dog that hung from a branch.

'Congratulations,' R'li said. 'We'll eat well for the next three days at least.'

Jack Cage's face twisted with disgust. 'You're not going to eat a *dog?* You don't expect *me* to eat it, do you?'

Polly turned a cheerful face to him. 'I'll eat anything to keep alive. Anyway, I don't mind. In fact, I like dog meat. My mother used to catch dogs and cook them for us. She didn't want me to grow up with the dietary prejudices of you Christians. And, of course, the coven always had dogs during the moon feasts.'

'It's not as if he's somebody's pet,' R'li said. 'He is a wild and dangerous animal.'

'No!' Jack said.

'But,' R'li continued, 'you make pets out of your unicorns and gagglers and other animals, then eat them. I've seen it happen on your farm more than once.'

'No!'

'Starve, then,' Polly said.

'You dog-eaters!' he snarled, and he walked off. Two hours later, he had seen nothing. Finally he settled for the balls of a wild totumtree. They made an unsatisfactory meal. Unlike that of their domestic cousins, their fruit had tough meat and thin, acid-tasting milk. But they did fill his stomach.

Returning, he found the two women munching on flesh that had been roasted over a small and comparatively smokeless fire. Silently Polly held out a piece to him. He sniffed; it did have an attractive odor. But his stomach turned.

'Maybe we'll find something else tomorrow,' R'li said. She was at least sympathetic, but Polly was grinning at him as if she thought him a fool.

Three days and nights passed. Jack refused the meat offered him three times daily by R'li. He ate totumtree balls and with each succeeding day, looked more desperately for barefox, mountain unicorn, and wild gagglers. Several times he sighted members of each kind, but they eluded him. He was getting weaker and shaky, and his stomach was turning sour from the fruit.

On the evening of the third day, while squatting by the supper fire, he cut himself off a piece of meat. R'li's expression did not change. Polly grinned, but she must have known from his glare that she would be better off if she said nothing. He wolfed the meat down, and so great was his hunger, it tasted better than anything he had ever eaten. A moment later, however, he was retching in the bushes.

That night, he arose and unwrapped the petticoat in which Polly was keeping the last of the cooked meat. He ate it, fought for a few seconds with his rising stomach, and quelled it. His dreams were bad that night, and he awoke irritable and with a bad taste in his mouth. But when Polly killed another dog that day, a bitch, he ate heartily.

'You're a man now,' Polly said, 'A more complete one, anyway.'

The following day, he had luck in his hunting. He speared a unicorn as she trotted down a forest path with two colts behind her. He had been downwind, and she must have been in a hurry to get wherever she was going. She did not seem to have the normal caution of a wild animal. The spear went into her side, and she turned with such force that she tore the shaft from his grasp. He leaped on her back and stabbed her in the side until she fell to the ground. Unfortunately, she fell on his leg. His bones were not broken, but he limped for several days thereafter.

In addition to the meat, the unicorn furnished sinews from which to make bow strings. Jack moved the sharp horn and attached it to a shaft of wood to make a spear. They spent several days fashioning arrows, arrowheads, bows, and quivers. It took them six days to cure the skin for the quivers and the sinews for the strings. R'li made it evident that she was impatient to get moving, but she admitted that they would need the weapons.

The meat was cut into strips and smoked. This process

necessarily involved much odor and smoke, and predators came. At two different times, tailbears came sniffing around the camp. Jack and the two women loosed some of their precious arrows. Although the bears were hit, they were not killed. One, after a short charge, changed his mind and fled. The others left the neighborhood as soon as they felt the first arrow in them.

The wild dogs were more dangerous. They came in packs of from six to twenty. They would sit down out of arrow range and gaze hungrily at the camp, the meat strung from the tree branches, and at the man and women. Jack walked out toward them. Some would retreat, while others circled to get behind him. Then R'li and Polly got close enough to shoot several. The other dogs would tear the wounded or dead apart and devour them. After a while, they would move on.

'I hope they never catch us in the open,' R'li said. 'Or take us by surprise. They're very quick and very clever.'

'I understand they're nothing to fear compared with the mandrakes and the werewolves,' Polly said. 'Those are half-human and much more intelligent than dogs.'

'Not to mention the dragons,' Jack said. 'We'll take them one at a time, if you please.'

They broke camp and resumed skirting the lower half of the Phul. The terrain became steeper, but it was still heavily forested. Only by walking in the stream itself could they avoid the thick brush. This method was impossible for more than short stretches because their feet and legs froze in the icy waters. Moreover, after two days, the little cascades became more frequent and were higher.

'We'd better abandon the stream anyway,' Jack said. 'If anyone caught us in it, they could shoot down from the banks.'

R'li did not argue. It was time to leave the brook. To get to the Argulh Valley, they had to quit climbing. They must circle the mountain at this level.

A little while later, Jack remarked that the path they were following was remarkably smooth.

'There's a road of the Arra buried beneath the forest soil, R'li said. 'It follows the mountain slope for quite a while and curves around until it ends there.' She indicated an enormous outcropping five hundred feet above them.

'There's a large plateau there, and on it the ruins of a city of the Arra.'

'I'd like to see it,' he answered. 'It wouldn't delay us too much if we took a side trip, would it?'

She hesitated, then said, 'It's something to see. No one should miss it. But there are enough dangers for us in the miles we do have to travel. I hate to add to them.'

'I've always heard so much about the Arra and their great cities,' he said. 'I've always wanted to see one. If I'd known that there was one up there, I'd have gone up a long time ago.'

'It's not forbidden country for you humans for no reason,' she said. 'Very well, if you must. Actually, I would like to see it again. But we must be careful.'

Polly O'Brien did not object. Indeed, she seemed eager. Jack asked her why her eyes shone at the thought, why she suddenly bubbled so much. 'It's said that the cities of the Arra have many buried secrets. If I could get my hands on something like that . . . '

'Don't get too excited,' R'li said. 'These ruins have been picked over many times.'

The 'path' they were following slowly curved up around the mountain, then abruptly took a less gentle turn. Now they were going in the opposite direction and were about a hundred feet higher than they had been when they decided to stay on it. Although they had been talking, they never let their voices rise above a loud whisper. And they kept their eyes open and their bows strung in one hand. It was R'li who first detected the face behind the leaves of a bush about twenty yards to their left. A second later, Jack also saw it.

'Walk as if you had seen nothing,' he said. 'But watch. I think the face belonged to Gill White. One of Ed Wang's boys.'

A few seconds later, he said harshly, 'Drop!' He hurled himself to the ground, with the two women only a fraction of a second behind him. Something *thunked* into the bole of a tree on their right. It became apparent: a quivering arrow.

There was a yell a little behind and above them. Men appeared from behind trees and bushes. Six men, among whom was Ed Wang.

Jack scrambled up, an arrow fitted to his string, and let fly. Three of the men cast themselves down, but the other three continued to draw their bows. Jack had hurled himself down again as soon as he had fired. He did not see his shaft strike, but he heard the agonized yell of one of the archers.

The two women rose as soon as the three arrows from Wang's group whistled overhead, and they shot. Neither struck their targets, but the men were unnerved and took refuge behind trees. Apparently they had expected only Jack to put up any dangerous resistance.

'Run!' Jack said, and he set the example. As he did so, he tried to search both sides of the forest path, for Ed might have planted some more men there for ambush. It did not seem likely. As he remembered, Ed had only had five men with him when he left the cadmi.

The path took another sudden turn, and they were going in the opposite direction and on a steeper slope. R'li, behind him, said, 'The ruins are only about two hundred yards away. There are many places to hide there. I know the place fairly well.'

Jack, running along the side of the path, could look down through the trees. There were men there, toiling up the mountainside. They were trying to short-cut to intercept the three, but they would have done much better to stick to the road. He looked behind him, saw no one, and slowed to a fast walk. No use burning himself out and getting out of breath.

R'li had stopped. 'Where's Polly?'

'I don't know where the little bitch is. Damn her! What's she up to now?'

'I think she dropped back to take some more potshots,' she said. 'She's courageous, whatever else she might be. Though I think it's part madness.'

'She wants revenge on Ed Wang,' he said. 'But I didn't think she'd risk getting herself killed for it.'

He decided not to go back to look for her. She'd made a foolish move, and he was not going to put R'li's life in jeopardy because of her.

'Damn her! If they take her alive, they'll rape her to death. I know what Ed planned for her!'

They rounded another turn, and they were on the plateau. The ruins were before them. And above them.

Even in his concern with their danger, he was awed. It must have been a cyclopean metropolis when it had been intact, before some cataclysm had tumbled it. There were a few buildings still half erect, and these towered several hundred feet high. They were constructed of tremendous blocks of granite and basalt, each a fifty-foot cube. The façades must once have been overlaid with a thin layer of some plaster or other material. Where it still remained, the material showed bright colors. Murals must have been painted there, for there were portions of scenes. Most numerous were creatures that looked like ursucentaurs, like the being that Kliz had portrayed in his painting. There were also men – horstels, rather – serving the Arra. And there were other semihuman beings, creatures that ressembled men but had brutish faces and hairy skins.

R'li said, 'The Arra transported others here as their slaves. Their descendants went completely back to savagery or even lower after the blowup. They are the things you call mandrakes and werewolves. Be careful. Some may be living in these ruins.'

'Where the hell is Polly?' he said, then fell silent as yells came from the trees below on the slope. The naked figure of the girl burst out of the forest, and she was running up the road. A moment later, four men appeared about a hundred yards behind her.

'Looks like she got one,' Jack said. 'But she missed Ed.'

He told R'li to get behind one of the huge blocks lying on the ground. He took a position behind another and waited. If the men were stupid enough to follow her closely on to the plateau, they could be disposed of with a few shots. He hoped they were.

But Polly trotted up to them, took a place by him, and they waited in vain. Ed Wang was not going to be trapped.

Polly had caught her breath by then. She said, 'They must be working their way up the slope. They'll slip in among the ruins someplace farther down.'

Jack did not want to have them behind him. He called to R'li, and the three trotted into the ruins. They threaded between the fallen structures, sometimes forced to take wide detours around vast heaps. To avoid being silhouetted if they climbed over the blocks, they stuck to ground level.

During one of their stops to watch and listen, R'li said, 'Quiet! I think . . . ' She got down on the ground and placed her ear next to it.

Jack felt the hairs of his neck prickle, and a coldness ran over his skin. The place was so silent. There was not even a wind; the harsh cries of the slashlarks, always heard in the forest, were absent. Yet, if he remembered correctly, they had been present only a minute ago.

R'li arose. She said, in child-talk, "*Thrruk.*"

'More than one?' he said.

'I think only one. She might just be passing through. Or she might be Mar-Kuk looking for the manling who has her thumb.'

'If she'll go away happy, I'll give it back to her,' he said. 'No hard feelings on either part.'

'Don't give it to her,' Polly said, 'If she shows up, threaten to destroy it. She won't know how you can do that, but she won't take the chance.'

'Polly's right,' R'li said.

She suggested that the best plan would be to go to the other, or back, side of the ruins. They could skirt the edge of the plateau for a while, then descend into the Argulh Valley. The path down was not one that she would take if she had a choice. But it would be safer than trying to return to the original road.

The city was vast. It was approximately two hours to dusk before they reached its northern limits. Abruptly, the last of the fallen blocks gave way to a level and treeless plain. This, empty of vegetation except for knee-high grass and a few winnybushes, extended for half a mile. Then, it broke. The Argulh Valley lay below, but they could see only the opposite side. Above it was the twenty-thousand-foot-high face of the Plel Massif.

For about half an hour, the three walked along the blocks. Jack felt nervous about crossing the plain while it was still day. R'li stopped them and said, 'The path starts there. Where that cone-shaped boulder sticks up over the edge of the drop-off.'

'Hour and a half until sundown,' he said. 'We'll rest.'

'The path is called so only by courtesy,' the siren replied. 'It's bad enough when you've light to see it by. By night . . . I don't know. We might very easily fall. But if we can get down a little way by the light, we can rest for the night on a ledge. Moreover, the ledge is easily defended.'

Jack sighed and said, 'All right. But let's run that half mile to the drop-off.'

They kept their bows in their hands while they sprinted. No sooner had they taken a few steps than they heard a cry behind them. Jack looked behind him and saw Ed Wang and his three followers running out from behind a stone block.

R'li wailed, 'We'll have to take a stand by the drop-off! If we go down the path now, they can drop rocks on us or shoot us! We'd be helpless!'

Jack said nothing but kept running. He was stopped by a great bellow that could only have come from the massive throat of a dragon. The two women also stopped and turned to look. The creature was Mar-Kuk, for she was missing a thumb.

Now the pursuers were pursued. They ran frantically towards the three who had lately been their quarry. Ed waved his bow and shouted. Although they could not hear what he was saying above the roars of the thing behind him, they guessed the sense. He wanted to join his forces with theirs and make a common stand against the dragon.

'Let them join us,' Jack said. 'It may be our only chance.'

One of Ed's men, Al Merrimoth had fallen behind the others. Mar-Kuk steadily overtook him. Then Merrimoth pitched forward. He rolled over to face the monster, threw his hands over his face, and hence did not see the great foot that descended on him and crushed out his life.

Given grace by Mar-Kuk's pause to take care of their comrade, Ed Wang and his friends reached their goal. They were sobbing for breath, but they turned and ranged themselves by the side of Jack and the two women. R'li said, 'Let me try to talk to her first.'

She stepped forward and called out in child-talk, 'Mar-Kuk! I invoke the trucespeech of the cadmus folk! May your mother and your grandmothers to the beginning of the Great Egg curse you and reject you if you fail to honor it!'

Mar-Kuk stopped running, her legs rigid and her body and tail bending back to keep from falling forward on her face. Her huge feet slid through the grass for several yards before she managed to brake to a stop.

'I honor the trucespeech,' she said in her incredibly deep voice. 'But only for the allotted time.'

'What do you want?' R'li said, although she knew well enough and the dragon knew she knew.

'What do I want?' Mar-Kuk's voice soared up until it almost became a soprano screech. 'By the Blessed Inside-out Egg, I want my thumb! And I want the body of the man who has defiled me by cutting it off and keeping it next to his evil male flesh!'

'He'll return it to you so that you may ritually cleanse yourself and return to the well-lit womb of the Grandest Mother when you die. But only if you swear to go away and never to harm him or those you see with him. You must swear by the Utmost Pain the Grandest Mother endured when she laid the Eight-Cornered Egg of the First Male.'

Mar-Kuk's jaw dropped, and she blinked. Her hands clasped and she clenched them against each other.

R'li said quietly to Jack, 'I don't think she'll do it. If she swears, then she'll be unable to harm you without condemning herself to a cold shadowy motherless hell. No *Thrruk* has ever broken that oath. But if she does swear, then she still may not go to her idea of heaven. Ritual cleansing, in this case at least, will take years. And if she should happen to die before the rituals were completed, she'd be doomed.'

'At least, she'd have a chance then.'

'I hope that's the conclusion she'll come to,' said R'li. She dropped her voice even lower and told him what to do. He nodded, then began to walk, with as casual a manner as he could adopt under the circumstances, towards the edge of the plateau. He did not turn his head to see what was going on behind him. But he could imagine Mar-Kuk's eyes on him and her indecision. When he was within a few yards of the edge, he heard a great cry. Wheeling, he saw that the dragon had made up her mind. She was charging toward him.

R'li and Polly ran to one side. Their bows were held away from their bodies, so that R'li must have told Polly what to expect. However, Ed and his two men made a mistake. They held their ground until they had loosed three shafts, two of which struck her. Both bounced off the thick hide.

The men then turned to run, but two of them were too slow. Mar-Kuk changed her course slightly; her long tail flicked out. Ed escaped, but the other two were hurled to the ground. Their bones splintered with a cracking sound.

She was a terrifying creature to see, so terrifying that Jack almost lost his nerve and tried to escape over the edge of the cliff and onto the 'path'. But R'li had insisted that he must hold firm. If he did not, they would all be lost, for Mar-Kuk's rage would be all-destructive.

He stood at the very lip of the drop-off and held the thumb at arm's length over the abyss. All he had to do was to open his hand, and the thumb would drop all the four thousand feet to the bottom.

Again, Mar-Kuk braked herself and slid on the grass. This time she only managed to come to a halt a few feet from Jack Cage.

Her bellow rang out. 'Don't do it'

Jack shook his head and spoke loudly and slowly in child-talk. 'If you kill me or force me to drop this, Mar-Kuk, your thumb will be lost forever to you. I doubt very much that you could find it. It'd take you far too long to get to the bottom of the valley. You can't go down the cliffside here; you're too big. And the chances are that the animals would have eaten it, anyway, before you could get there.'

She broke into a series of meaningless syllables. He guessed she was swearing in the original language of the dragons. R'li had told him that the superior prestige of horstel speech had long ago made the dragons adopt that in place of their own. But they retained certain phrases from the lost tongue for ritual and cursing.

Jack tried to smile as if he were master of the situation and found her amusing. That columnar bulk and horrendous face and the wrath that filled her reduced his effort to a brief flicker at the corner of his lips. His knees were shaking, and the hand that held the thumb quivered.

R'li said, 'We'll give it back to you when we reach the Idoh Pass. Provided that you don't try to come after us then. And you must promise to accompany us and protect us.'

Mar-Kuk gargled with frustration, then swallowed it. 'All right.'

Jack continued to hold the thumb out until R'li had made the dragon give a formal oath. Then, his arm weary, he walked back to the unicorn-hide bag and put the thumb within. Mar-Kuk eyed it, but she made no move, then or thereafter, to seize it.

Jack and R'li dragged the bodies to the edge and tumbled them over. Much as he wanted to bury them, he had no digging tools.

Mar-Kuk complained that she was being deprived of easy meat. She became silent when R'li explained that they had gotten rid of the corpses to keep from attracting mandrakes. Jack wondered what manner of beasts these could be to make even the colossus Mar-Kuk want to avoid them.

Ed stood glowering at them, his bow and knife at his feet, where Polly had ordered him to drop them. She stood a few yards away with her arrow cocked, ready to fire.

R'li's voice came from behind Jack. 'You had best kill him now.'

He was surprised. 'That doesn't sound like you!'

'You can't release him with his weapons. If you do, he'll be trying to stab us while we're asleep. He *hates*. If you turn him out without weapons . . .'

'He can make new ones, just as he made those . . .'

'Not a chance. Didn't you hear what Polly said? She hates, too, and she'll go after him. He'll die as no one should, in the most agonizing and the slowest way. I know those witches; I know Polly.'

'It's too bad I didn't kill him when he was after us,' he said. 'But I can't now, not in cold blood.'

'You killed a mad dog once. He was your pet; you loved him. You don't love Ed.'

'I'm in the wilderness with two of the most vicious bitches that ever hounded a man!' he said. He walked away, but he knew that she spoke truly and that she spoke out of humanity. Besides, Ed had tried to murder all of them and more than once.

R'li walked over slowly to Polly and stood by her for a moment. Jack watched them. What was she up to? They seemed to be talking about nothing serious. Polly was laughing.

Suddenly R'li struck. Her fist took Polly on the side of her jaw, and the woman crumpled. She fell to her knees and hands, where she remained on all fours for a few seconds. That was all the siren needed. She scooped up Polly's bow and arrow, fitted the shaft to the string, and aimed at Ed.

He came out of his freeze, yelled, and started to run. There was only one place he could possibly take refuge, over the edge of the plateau. R'li's arrow caught him in the back just as he started to throw himself to the ground to halt his forward speed. Undoubtedly he had intended to continue the roll with the hope that the path, which he had only heard them mention, would be directly below. But he staggered forward, yelling, the shaft sticking from his left shoulderblade, and went headlong over. His yell floated up for some time. Then, silence.

Jack came running. Polly got up, rubbing her jaw, and said, 'You bitch! You cheated me!'

'He's dead now,' R'li said. 'Forget about him.'

'I won't forget about you!'

'I'll tell Mar-Kuk to keep an eye on you,' R'li said calmly.

All four went back into the ruins. Mar-Kuk, who was leading, stopped with an exclamation. Jack followed her pointing hand – the thumbless one – and saw the fresh droppings of a large animal.

'Mandrake!' she said.

'They coil around in a characteristic pattern and always have that little tip,' R'li explained to Jack. 'Well, we'll have to pick a good place for certain. Hurry! The sun'll be down in a few minutes.'

'Here's a nice hole,' Mar-Kuk said. She stood sniffing in front of a square entrance formed by a tumble of the great blocks. Within the darkness was a room large enough for all. At a few words from R'li, the dragon went off to search for firewood. The others entered their lodging for the night. An examination showed that the way by which they had come was the only entrance.

Mar-Kuk returned fifteen minutes later, her arms full of branches, twigs, and a sizable log. She placed the stuff on the ledge stone, squeezed her bulk through, and then arranged the wood. With flintstones and shavings, Jack soon had a fire blazing. It burned completely across the entrance and made a fine fire except that occasionally the wind blew smoke in. They cooked some unicorn and ate. Mar-Kuk downed most of it, said, 'Never fear, little ones. I'll find another el [child-talk for unicorn] for you tomorrow.'

'How can she go with us?' Jack whispered to R'li. 'She can't get down that trail.'

'We'll go with her the long way around. It'll take more time, but it'll be much safer. Why are you whispering?'

He gestured with his head at the bulk behind them. 'She makes me nervous.'

R'li kissed Jack on the cheek and patted his back. Polly said, 'I'm sorry my presence has inconvenienced you two so much. But don't let me bother you. Have at it. I'll enjoy watching, and I might even ask for leavings.'

'You're a vile bitch!' Jack said.

'I'm an honest one,' she replied. 'But I meant what I said. I've seen you hugging her and kissing her and fondling those wonderful breasts when you thought I wasn't looking. You two must have known each other for some time. Why isn't she pregnant? Or doesn't she want to be?'

Jack gasped and said, 'Wha – what? You know humans and horstels can't have children.'

Polly laughed loudly and for a long time. Mar-Kuk, in the rear of the chamber, began to stir uneasily. At last, Polly quit.

She said, 'Hasn't your love told you the truth of that story the fat priests give you? Of course, you two can have a baby! There are thousands of hybrids living right now, most of them in Socinia.'

'Is this true, R'li? Why didn't you tell me?'

'Jack, we had little time together. We did a lot of talking, but it was mostly about our love for each other. We couldn't cover everything you might be interested in. Besides, you were in no danger of making me pregnant. The Wiyr can have babies only when they want them. When the population regulators tell them they can, rather. We have always kept a close watch on the balance of birth and death. You humans don't. That's why you are outnumbering us and are so hungry to take over our lands.'

'We witches have known how to prevent conception for some time, too,' Polly said. 'You take certain herbs, mix them, swallow them at certain times.'

R'li peered out into the darkness, past the blaze. The moon had not yet come up. Outside was a clear space of about twenty yards and then a towering pile of blocks.

'I think it's time to tell you the true story of the Wiyr, or the horstels, or the cadmen, or the sirens and satyrs, or the dogeaters or any of the many names you call us. The story that your State and Church have hidden from you. Although, possibly, they may be ignorant of much of it themselves.

'Jack, the Wiyr, as we call ourselves, that is, the People, also come from Earth.'

Jack did not reply.

'It's true, Jack. Our ancestors were brought to this planet some four thousand years ago. Darian years, which closely correspond to Terrestrial years. At that time, the Arra had a flourishing colony on this planet. They abducted human beings from Earth and used them as slaves or servants. Not that they needed slaves to serve them, for their machines could do that. But they wanted other *lower* but intelligent beings as prestige items and as pets.

'They also brought sapients from the planets of other stars. These were the ancestors of the present-day mandrakes and werewolves. The dragons have always been here. They were a primitive group that were too big and dangerous to be domesticated. So they were kept on a reservation.

'About two thusand years ago another interstellar culture, the Egzwi, warred with the Arra. They used a weapon that exploded or disintegrated all surface iron. Also, I believe, certain other metals. The surviving Arra deserted their colony. The Egzwi never landed. And, of the four sapient species left behind, the human beings alone managed to struggle back out of savagery. We made certain of that. We hunted and harried the mandrakes and the werewolves, as you call them, until they survived only in mountainous areas we didn't want.'

'What proof do you have for this story?' Jack said. 'If you're human, why do you have the horsetails and the yellow and orange eyes?'

'One theory is that we were mutated by the radiations from the explosion of iron and other metals. Another is that the Arra deliberately mutated us. We do know that they bred us for certain physical qualities.

'However, we also have our traditions. These might not be enough to prove what I say. Perhaps we could have come from a different planet. But there's another factor. Language.'

'Yours is absolutely different.'

'Adult-talk, yes. That's Arra speech, which all slaves had to learn. It's a code or clichè language, or, better, a mnemonic tongue. You use brief code words that contain the meaning of whole sentences or phrases.

'But child-talk is a descendant of the original speech we used on Earth. The slaves were allowed to use it among themselves, and they clung to it as a reminder of their once free estate. After the blowup, it came to be a marker of the distinction between the ruling class of the Wiyr and the others. You assumed that all horstels used adult-talk, but that's not true. It's spoken only by the aristocrats.

'However, the important thing is that our child-talk and most of the languages used by the Earthlings who were dropped off by that later Arra ship . . . well, they come from the same root speech. Our scholars recorded them before English came to be the dominant, and then the only, language of the descendants of you *tarrta*, or latecomers. English, German, Icelandic, Spanish, Portuguese, Bulgarian, Albanian, Gaelic Irish, Italian, Greek, and your liturgical language Latin. Only Turkish, Chinese, and Croatan seemed not to be related to yours.'

'I find that hard to believe,' he said.

'Darling, I would think you'd be eager to believe it! It proves our common origin.'

'I don't know. I can't see any similarity between English,

horstel, and Latin. Except what the priests say we borrowed from Latin.'

'I'm not a scholar, either. But I know a little of it, and I can take you to learned men of my own people who know a lot. Besides, at two different times, priests of your own kind came to recognize the similarities. One was threatened with ex-communication if he didn't keep quiet. Another went cadmus.'

'All right. I'm not angry, as you seem to think. Just dazed.'

'Our scholars could give you hundreds of examples. I'll give you a few. For instance, you have the insulting word *swine*. You've never seen the animal that was the original swine; neither have I. But it was a dirty nasty beast. Our word, with the same pejorative meaning, is *suth*. At the time of the blow-up, it was *sus*. It's related to the Latin *suinus* and the German *schwein*. All three words came from the same word or related words, of the mother tongue.

'Take O-Reg, the Blind King. *O* is a loanword from Arra. Originally, it stood for a whole phrase, the meaning of which had to do with a lack of foresight or insensitivity. But it means in child-talk, blind. *Reg*, however, was a word the Wiyr brought with them from Earth. It's related to the Latin *rex*, the genitive singular form of which is *regis*.'

'I don't see it.'

'*Thrruk* comes from the same ancestral form as your *dragon*, which you borrowed from the French, which got it from Latin, which borrowed it from Greek. Then there's our word for mother: *metrra*.

'Oh, I could go on for quite a while, even with my limited knowledge. Let's see. What does *were* in werewolf mean?'

'I never thought about it.'

'It means *man*. A *were*wolf is a *man*wolf. You *tarrta* called those creatures that because they seemed to look as if they're half-human and half-wolf. The point is, *were* is descended from the same common ancestor as the Latin *vir*, which means man and was once pronounced *wir*. Both words are cousins to *wiyr*, our name for *man* or *folk* or *people*.'

'It's hard for me to believe.'

'I didn't either until they explained to me the system of sound changes that must have taken place among the various families of speech descended from the original. They had it all worked out. Not just for a few, which might be attributed to coincidence. No, for thousands.'

'For instance,' Polly said, 'their word for the male organ and ours for a male gaggler, and also for the bad word for the male organ, seem remarkably alike, don't you think?'

'It's no coincidence,' R'li said.

'I always thought the priests said it was a horstel word, and that's why we shouldn't use it.'

Both R'li and Polly laughed. Jack was glad that he could step back into the darkness to hide his flush. He bumped into Mar-Kuk; she rumbled; he stepped swiftly forward. The dragon hissed and rose as far as she could beneath the low ceiling.

'*Sssss!* Silence! There's something out there!'

The three fitted arrows to their bows and gazed out into the darkness and the flickering cast by the fire. 'What do you think it is?' R'li said quietly.

'I can't smell them, but I heard them. More than one. I wish I were out of this little hole. I feel trapped.'

There was a concert of screams, some yowls, and five or six dark bodies appeared before the opening. In the light of the fire were creatures with man-shaped bodies covered with long dark hair. Their massive arms were longer than a human being's, however, and their shoulders were much broader and their chests enormous.

On top of a squat neck was a face covered with white hair. Their jaws were heavy and protruding, and their noses were huge and seemingly covered with cartilage or, perhaps, horn. The ears stood out at right angles to the heads and were almost square. The eyebrows were thick and black, contrasting with the white hair of the face. The eyes themselves were very large and orange in the reflection of the light, like an animal's.

They thrust long wooden spears with fire-hardened points into the opening. Those inside released their bows; the arrows thudded into three chests. Then the things were gone.

'Mandrakes!' R'li said.

Mar-Kuk said that she had to get out. She could not stand being caught inside. The others did not argue but moved around behind her. With one sweep of her tail she scattered the fire from the ledge and onto the ground outside. As swiftly as she could manage her great body, she squeezed through the opening. Halfway out, she bellowed as six dark bodies fell on her from above. She give a kick and propelled herself the rest of the way, with the mandrakes clinging to her. Before rising, she rolled over and crushed two of the attackers. The others scrambled away in time but returned at once to attack. They were joined by at least ten more running up from the shadows of the blocks, where they had been hiding.

Jack Cage and the women shot whenever they had a chance. But Mar-Kuk whirled around so much and rushed back and forth so swiftly, they could get only three good attempts. Two struck their marks, though not fatally, for the mandrakes ran off howling.

Suddenly the attackers had had enough, more than enough. They quit their futile stabbing with wooden spears or beating with clubs or biting with teeth, and fled. Mar-Kuk chased one group down the avenue formed by the piles of stone blocks. Jack could hear their screaming and the dragon's bellowings for some time. Then they faded into the distance.

They took turns at sentinel duty. Mar-Kuk did not return until dawn. She looked tired but content and very well fed. When they continued their journey, she picked up one of the dead mandrakes, saying that she would keep it for breakfast the next day.

All that day, with only several brief rests, they walked. By noon they had left the ruins behind them, and they now followed along the edge of the plateau. When dusk came, they had climbed down several hills and were halfway down the slope of a small mountain. R'li calculated that they could get to the bottom of the Argulh Valley by mid-afternoon of the next day.

'It's at least sixty miles across, rough, and heavily wooded, as you saw from the plateau. It's infested with everything dangerous to man. Even the unicorns are bigger and more aggressive. But with Mar-Kuk along, I don't think we have too much to fear,' R'li said.

By noon of the third day, they were almost halfway across. Nothing had offered to molest them, and they had not even had to hunt for themselves. Mar-Kuk had cornered a unicorn in a little canyon and killed it for meat. They made a small fire on the bank of a wide, shallow stream and sat down to eat. Mar-Kuk shifted around uneasily for a few minutes, then said that she had to be going for a while.

'Some of your sisters are in the neighborhood?' R'li said.

'Yes, I want to gossip with them. Also, to tell them that they must spread the word that you are to be left alone. If they don't, they'll have me to deal with.'

'I hope she won't be gone long,' R'li said. 'But I'm afraid she will. Dragons chatter on as much as human females.'

An hour passed. Jack became impatiient. R'li sat quietly, her eyes fixed on a stick set upright in the sand before her. Apparently she had gone into a trance. This irritated Jack because she refused to pay any attention to him then. Afterward, she could not explain to his satisfaction what she was thinking. Polly lay sprawled out in the grass, her arms behind her head, in a consciously provocative position. For the past few days, she had been eying him with an expression that was anything but unreadable. Also, her comments had been getting bolder. R'li ignored both the looks and remarks. Jack, although he disliked Polly, even detested her, felt guilty. The rigors of the trip had not tired him so much that he did not feel an ever-increasing pressure. The lack of privacy and R'li's strange disinclination had prevented him from doing something about it.

Once, when he was briefly alone with her, he had asked her why she was so cold.

'I'm not. But I'm under a tabu for fourteen days. Every woman of the Wiyr observes chastity for that period, the time depending upon her birthday. It's in honor of the Goddess in her aspect of the divine huntress.'

Jack had thrown his hands up in the air. All his life he had lived with the cadmen, and yet he knew nothing of their ways.

'What about me?' he had said. 'Am I supposed to suffer during this holy observance?'

'There's Polly.'

He was flabbergasted. 'Do you mean that you wouldn't care?'

'No. I'd care very much. But I'd never say anything about it. I'm forbidden to do so. And I'd understand . . . somewhat . . . I think.'

'I wouldn't touch that vicious little bitch if she were the last woman alive.'

R'li smiled. 'You do exaggerate. And you underestimate your desires. Besides, it would then be your duty to propagate.'

Later, he decided that R'li could not actually compel him to practice chastity, but she had made it plain that she would resent it very much if he did not. Thank God, he told himself, he was not tempted. But he wished that Polly would not make it so obvious that she felt a strong need, too. He had reactions he could not help.

Angry, he nudged R'li's buttock with his toe and said, 'Let's get going. Mar-Kuk can trail us easily enough.'

R'li blinked her eyes and said, 'Why the hurry?'

Jack flicked a glance at Polly and said, 'I just can't take this waiting. That's all.'

R'li also looked at Polly, who had not changed her posture. She said, 'Very well.'

A half hour later, Jack wished that he had exercised more control. The more distance they put between themselves and Mar-Kuk, the more they increased their vulnerability. But he was too stubborn to admit that he had been wrong. Fifteen minutes later, he admitted to himself that it would be stupid to continue any longer.

He stopped and said, 'Let's wait for her here. I made a mistake.'

The women did not comment. R'li fixed the stick in the soft ground and sat down cross-legged to stare at its tip. Polly resumed her legs-open, hands-beneath-her-head position. They were back where they had been, except that now their protector was farther away. He began pacing again.

He stopped. Polly sat upright, her eyes wide, her head cocked. R'li came out of her trance. Somebody was running through the brush and making no attempt to be silent. Mar-Kuk?

A male horstel ran out of the forest and continued across the stream. He was about fifty yards away and did not see them.

R'li said, 'Mrrn!' as Jack recognized her brother.

There was an explosion of gunfire. Halfway across the stream, Mrrn staggered and fell forward. He rose again, went a few steps, and fell face down in the water. His body began to float downstream.

R'li had screamed when her brother was hit. Jack said, 'Into the woods!'

They picked up their weapons and bags and started to run toward the nearest trees. Before they reached them, they halted. Several men, all holding firearms, had stepped out. Among them was Chuckswilly.

He smiled and said, 'Your brother was looking for you, and we were trailing him. Now we should all be happy, for each found what he was seeking. Or am I wrong? Perhaps you aren't happy to see me?'

'I thought I'd killed you,' Jack said.

'You did give me quite a bump on the head. I suffered from it the next few days while I was in the Slashlark jail.'

'Jail!'

'Yes. The government had decided that the time wasn't ripe to attack the horstels. The Queen was angry about the Cage cadmi. She had me arrested, and I was to be put on trial as testimony of her good intentions toward the Wiyr. However, several of my friends broke into the jail late the third night and set me free. I decided that my usefulness was ended in Dyonisa, so I set out for Socinia, my native land. I ran into this patrol, and a little later, we encountered Mrrn and a couple of his friends. I imagine they were looking for you.'

Jack put his arm around R'li's waist and held her close to him. She was pale, and her face was set. Poor darling! To have lost her father and brother in such a short time!

'You're a Socinian?' he said.

'An agent to provoke war between the horstel and Dyonisan. I may have seemed to fail at your farm, but I didn't. Every cadmus throughout the three nations is jumpy, ready to fight back. Other Socinians will cause more incidents. The whole continent will explode. All lands except mine, of course. We'll be prepared to march in after man and cadman have decimated each other.

'Now we must dispose of the problem you present. I'll be brief. Either you swear to go to Socinia, there to become citizens and to fight for it, or you die now.'

Several soldiers waded into the stream and dragged Mrrn onto the bank. He sat up and coughed until he had cleared the water from his nostrils and throat. The side of his head revealed blood seeping out from a shallow wound. The bullet had merely grazed his skull.

Chuckswilly repeated the offer he had made to Jack, R'li, and Polly.

Mrrn spat and said, 'My sister and I prefer death!'

'You're not very bright,' Chuckswilly said. 'If you were, you'd have promised to join us and then looked for a chance to escape later. But you're a horstel of the ruling class, and they don't lie. Or do they?'

He said to R'li, 'You can speak for yourself. You don't need to refuse simply because you are a Wiyr. Two of my men are of cadman descent. One is a hybrid. I'm a hybrid, too. Socinia is an example of the fact that the two cultures can fuse to make a harmonious third.'

'Why don't you let us go?' she answered. 'We are on our way to the Valley of the Thrruk. We intend to live there in peace and raise our children there. We can't harm you.'

He raised his eyebrows and stroked his mustache. He grinned and said, 'Live there in peace? Not for long. Socinia intends to conquer the valley, too. After we have disposed of Dyonisa, Croatania, and Farfrom.'

Scornfully she said, 'It's too well defended. You could lose a hundred thousand men and still not storm the pass!'

'What's the matter with horstel espionage? Haven't you heard of our big guns and powerful shells? They make the Dyonisan artillery look like toys. And we have great balloons, propelled by motors, which can fly above the pass and bomb the valley out. Or descend and discharge troops so powerfully armed they'll cut down your fighters as a farmer scythes weeds.'

R'li gasped and clung to Jack. Chuckswilly said, 'Well, which shall it be? You might as well know that if you refuse, you'll be turned over to my men. They're very horny just now; they've been in the wilderness too long.'

R'li asked for permission to speak to Jack privately. Chuckswilly agreed, but he had the hands of the two bound behind them and their ankles tied together.

'What shall we do?' she said.

'Agree to join. He himself said we'd probably do that and try to escape later.'

'You don't understand,' she said. 'We who are descended from the Blind Kings don't lie even to save our lives.'

'Damn it, I'm not asking you to be a traitor! Just play along! All right, don't lie. Avoid a direct answer. Tell Chuckswilly you'll do whatever I do. You know what my intentions are.'

'That would be trickery. It's indirect lying.'

'Do you want to die for nothing?'

'I don't think it's nothing,' she said stiffly. 'But I love you. You gave up much for me. All right, I'll do as you say.'

Jack called Chuckswilly to him. 'I'll join. R'li will do whatever I do.'

Chuckswilly grinned and said, 'She's not only beautiful, she's ambiguous. Very well. I'll untie your feet. For the moment, your hands will remain bound.'

As was to be expected, Polly O'Brien had already sworn an oath to live and die for Socinia. Chuckswilly told her that he knew more about her than she thought. She was joining as an expediency, but he expected that she would remain faithful to the oath. Why not? She loved a winner, and Socinia would be victorious. Once she got to his country, she'd see that.

Polly could even practice her religion openly, since Socinia had religious toleration. However, human sacrifice was forbidden. If she knew what was good for her, and he expected that she did, she would take no part in illegal rites. Several had, and they were now in prison mines and being worked to death.

Polly's only reply was to ask for a smoke.

Jack had recovered enough to notice that the soldiers were armed with firearms of a type he had never seen before. They were made of some 'plastic' material that was as strong as the rare iron. The bullets and the charges were enclosed in one package and were inserted through an opening in the breech. He asked Chuckswilly about them.

'One Socinian soldier has the firepower of ten Dyonisans and a hell of a lot more accuracy. Those round objects you see hanging from their belts are bombs three times as powerful as an equivalent Dyonisan bomb. Moreover, we can shoot them to a respectable distance with our rifles.

'If your dragon shows up, she won't stand a chance.'

Jack was startled at this disclosure. But a little thought showed him that Chuckswilly had seen her tracks with those of himself and the women.

The Socinian went to R'li's brother. 'I'm giving you one more chance. Your death will be for nothing. The culture of your people, of any non-Socinian, is doomed. We intend to smash the cadmi and make you horstels abandon your former mode of life. It was admirably suited for a very stable agricultural society, but it prevented technological advance. It has become a thing of the past.'

Chuckswilly turned to Jack and R'li. 'Make him realize that. Socinia will not be stopped. We must become as scientifically and technologically advanced as possible in as short a time as we can. The Arra have been here twice, and they, or somebody like them, will come here again. When they do, they will find themselves facing men who can give them a bloody fight, perhaps even defeat them. Men must not become slaves again. The Arra had space ships. We'll have those, too, someday. When we do, we'll carry the fight to the Arra.'

Jack became excited at this. Chuckswilly made sense. Many times he had wondered what would happen if the Arra did return. Once, he had asked Father Patrick about it. The priest had replied that the Lord would take care of them. If mankind were reduced to slavery again, man could benefit. He would be taught humility. Jack had not said so, but he had found the father's answer totally unsatisfactory.

'I won't take the slightest pleasure in killing you, Mrrn,' Chuckswilly said. 'In fact, it'll make me sick. But we have to be ruthless. There may not be enough time. The Arra ships could appear out of the sky today, and we'd be too late.'

'I would rather be dead than live as you do. I am a Wiyr, son of the Blind King and now the Blind King himself. No!'

Chuckswilly took a short-barreled firearm from a holster on his belt. He pointed it at Mrrn's forehead. His finger tightened, and a piece of the gun rose from behind the barrel. Then it fell, and the muzzle spat fire and noise. Mrrn fell backward onto the ground with a large hole just above his right eye.

R'li screamed and began sobbing.

Chuckswilly said to Jack, 'I could have forced you to prove your loyalty by asking you to execute him. But I am not inhumane. That would be too much.'

Jack did not reply. He could never have killed R'li's brother or anyone under such circumstances.

R'li spoke between her sobs. 'Chuckswilly, may I give my brother the rites of burial? He is the Blind King: he should not be left to rot in the open as a beast.'

'That involves removing his head and burning it, doesn't it? No, I'll have no smoke. I will bury him, but you can't go through the complete ritual. It'd take too long.'

The next moment, the soldiers were firing their guns. Three dragons had managed to get close to the group without being seen. Roaring, they charged out from the trees. The patrol fired point-blank, and one of the monsters went down at once, her belly blown apart. The other two, though wounded, kept coming on. Only Jack saw Mar-Kuk appear from the woods at the edge of the stream on the opposite side. The explosions of the guns, the shouts of the men, and the bellows of the dragons kept anyone from hearing the splash of her driving feet. So it was that she fell on them from behind and smashed four of the soldiers with a slash of her tail. Chuckswilly fired at her with his pistol and hit her three times. Jack slammed against him and knocked him to the ground. Mar-Kuk's tail swished over the space they had been occupying. By trying to put Chuckswilly out of action, Jack had also saved himself.

He was helpless now, with his hands tied behind his back, and could not prevent the man from getting to his feet again. Chuckswilly fired once more, hitting Mar-Kuk in her right arm. The hammer of his gun clicked, and he turned to run across the stream. Jack stuck out his legs and tripped him. Then Mar-Kuk picked Chuckswilly up and raised him high to hurl him against a tree.

Abruptly she collapsed. Her body made the ground quiver, and her head missed Jack by a few inches.

Only Polly and R'li were left standing, and R'li had her hands tied.

'Polly!' Jack called. 'Untie me!' He struggled to his feet and looked around. All the soldiers were either dead or wounded too badly to move. Chuckswilly was unconscious. Three of the dragons were dead. Mar-Kuk still breathed; her eyes were open and looking at Jack. Blood pumped from her belly, arm, head and the soft underside of the tip of her tail.

Polly had picked up her bow and fitted an arrow to it. Now she stood undecided.

For a few seconds, she was rigid with thought. Then she shrugged and placed her bow and arrow on the ground. In three minutes, she had collected the firearms and ammunition and stacked them beneath a tree. Next she removed a belt and holster from a corpse and strapped it around her waist. She examined a hand-gun, figured out how to reload and unload it, fired it once into the air, and placed the hand-gun in the holster.

Chuckswilly had regained consciousness. Groaning, he sat with his back against Mar-Kuk's side while he watched Polly. He said, 'Fortunes of war, heh? What now?'

'Just let us go on our way,' Jack said. 'We can't harm you now. You two do what you want to.'

Polly's reply was drowned by the great bleat of the dragon.

'My thumb! Give me my thumb! I am dying!'

'I promised it to her, Polly,' Jack said.

She hesitated, then shrugged and said, 'Why not? The dragons have worked with us witches before. I've nothing to lose.'

She opened the leather bag and removed the thumb. Mar-Kuk opened her hand to receive it, hugged it against her chest, and died a few minutes later.

By then, Chuckswilly had managed to stand up. 'Let them

go, Polly. They can't hurt Socinia. They'll regret not accepting my offer when we invade their hiding place. But they can have some happiness before we do that. They're last on the list.'

'Your word is my law,' Polly said. She untied the knots of the ropes binding the captives' hands. She backed away, keeping her eyes on them, and picked up a dead soldier's canteen and drank. The waters of the stream were still pink with the blood of a dragon whose charge had carried her to the bank before she collapsed.

Jack flexed his hands to get their circulation going again. He said, 'I hope you're not going to turn us loose without weapons?'

'No,' she said. 'I'm not as vindictive as you seem to think I am. You'll need arms going back to the cadmus just as much as you did getting here.'

Jack said that he did not understand. Polly jerked a thumb at R'li. 'You don't know the Wiyr very well, do you? She has to return home. Her father, brother, and uncle are dead. That means that she is now the head of her cadmi. She will be so until she dies or bears a son. It is her duty.'

Jack turned to R'li. 'This isn't true?'

R'li tried to speak, could not, and nodded her head.

'Damn it, R'li! There's nothing to go back to! Even if there were, you couldn't go! I left my duties behind when I left my people behind for you! You have to do the same for me!'

'As long as my father . . . uncle . . . Mrrn lived, I could go and do as I wished. I could even marry you, although my father argued a long time with me about it and said that I couldn't stay at our cadmus if I did. It would cause too much trouble with you *tarrta*. I had to go with you to the Thrruk.

'I could still do so as long as Mrrn was alive. But now . . .'

She broke into long, racking sobs, and only after some time did she control herself well enough to speak coherently.

'I have to. It's the custom. I can't forget them . . . my cadmus.'

Chuckswilly said, 'You're just beginning to find out, Jack Cage. They live by tradition and custom, and they will not deviate. They're stuck in the mud of the ages, enclosed in the stone form of their society. We Socinians intend to shatter that form.'

Jack said, his voice rising, 'I feel sick. Do you know how much I gave up for you, R'li?'

She nodded again, but her features hardened with a look he knew too well. Soft-voiced, soft-curved R'li could at times become granite.

'You have to go with me!' he shouted. 'I'm your husband; you must obey me!'

Poly laughed and said, 'Your wife is a horstel and the daughter of the Blind King.'

'We might not have to stay there forever,' R'li said pleadingly. 'If we could get the son of an O-Reg from another cadmus to accept the kingship, I could honorably retire.'

'Fat chance of that! You know that all hell may be loosed at any moment! I doubt very much if any horstel would venture this far from his cadmus at this time! Or leave it when it may need every fighting man it has!'

'Then I must go!'

Chuckswilly said, 'Do you want us to force her to come along with us? In a short time, there won't be any place for her to go back to.'

'No, I'll force no woman!' Jack said. He paused, struck with a frightening thought. Would Chuckswilly actually allow R'li or himself to return to Dyonisa? Chuckswilly could not take the chance that R'li might be able to inform the Dyonisan government of the threat of Socinia. He wondered what to do and in the middle of his indecision knew that he still loved R'li. Even her refusal to go with him had not changed that. Otherwise, why would he be caring whether or not she was killed?

Still, he was the man in this partnership, and she must go where he went.

As if Chuckswilly had been reading Jack's mind, he said, 'If you're thinking that I will have to kill R'li to keep her from talking, forget about it. She won't get a chance to talk. Even if the humans listened to her, they wouldn't believe a siren.'

There was little to say after that, but much to do. Chuckswilly showed all of them how to straighten out the little collapsible shovels the soldiers had carried and how to lock them. With these, they dug two graves, a small and a large one. The two men and Polly dragged the bodies to the shallow grave, rolled them in, and then heaped dirt over them. It took them awhile to gather enough large rocks and small boulders to pile over the dirt to keep the animals away. The dragons were left where they had fallen, except that the one that had fallen halfway into the stream was rolled out of it.

R'li insisted that she alone would dig her brother's grave. Before placing his body in it, she hacked off his head. The body was covered with dirt and rocks. Then, despite Chuckswilly's protests, she built a pyre of wood and burned the head. While the flames devoured the flesh, she prayed in child-talk and chanted in adult-talk. Afterward, she broke the half-charred skull into fragments with a stone and cast the pieces into the stream.

By then, the sun had passed the zenith. Chuckswilly had been getting more nervous with every minute. He looked at the smoke ascending, and his thoughts were plain to Jack and Polly. What enemies would be running toward them at sight of the pillar rising high for every eye in the valley?

Finally he said, 'We can't wait here any longer.'

He gave Jack and Polly a rifle, revolver, and bullets and showed them how to operate the guns. The extra weapons had been wrapped in leather and buried beneath a tree.

Jack gave R'li a last look. She was standing by the stream, her back to them and gazing out on the surface at the bone bits floating away or being pushed on the bottom by the current. For a second, he thought of making a last plea. But the set of her shoulders and his knowledge of her made him abandon the idea.

'Goodbye, R'li,' he said softly. He walked away to follow the others.

That night, after they had made camp and eaten, Chuckswilly said, 'You've probably agreed to join me because you hope to observe our secrets. Then you'll try to get out of the country and return to Dyonisa with your information. You won't get far. They won't believe a heretic, a siren-lover, any more than they would a horstel. You'd be burned at the stake after a very short trial.

'But I'm not worried about your spying. After you've been in Socinia, you'll see how hopeless the resistance of the humans and horstels would be even if they combined against us instead of slaughtering each other. You'll think about the Arra returning and how Socinia is this world's sole hope to fight them. You'll become a Socinian, if only to save your own people.'

Jack heard his words but did not reflect on them. He was thinking about R'li and wondering if she were safe. He ached within himself for her; tears crept down his cheeks.

For five days, they walked the forest path. Twice they had to use the firearms. Once to repel a pack of mandrakes; a second time, to discourage dragons. Then they were at the foot of a large mountain. It took them two days to get over that, a day to travel a small valley, three days to climb another mountain. The pass near its top was about five miles long. At its end, they came upon an ancient road of the Arra.

A Socinian garrison was stationed there in a small fort. Chuckswilly identified himself and told his story. The three got into a steam-powered wagon and were driven off down the road. The speedteller on a panel indicated that they were traveling at fifty miles an hour. Jack was apprehensive at first, but then he became exhilarated. He saw a giant balloon above them, and he cried out in wonder.

The countryside had many cadmi thrusting their ivory horns from the meadows. Chuckswilly told him that most of them were deserted, that everybody lived above ground now. 'We had a war of our own here,' he said. 'Human and the hybrid horman' – he chuckled – 'against the horstel who refused to give up his way of life.'

They had to slow down, for the traffic of 'steamers' began to get heavy. After several leagues' journey, they turned off to a fort. Here, Jack began his training as a soldier. He asked for and got service in the big armor-plated steamers called 'bears'. Those carried a cannon and several fast-firing, heavy-caliber firearms called 'crankers'. The operator rotated a crank that, in turn, revolved a cluster of ten barrels. As each barrel passed a certain point, a cartridge was slipped into the barrel from a disc and the ammunition was fired at the next position. It could shoot ten bullets per second.

There were many other marvels, but he did not get to see all of them. He was allowed to leave the training post only one day every fortnight. He did learn that much of the technological progress had come about because the Socinians had been fortunate enough to find a buried library of the Arra.

Winter came. Jack went through exercises and maneuvers on ice and through snow. Spring promised. His battalion was ordered out. It traveled down the same road by which he had entered. It went through the pass and into the Argulh Valley. Here, the old Arra road, buried under the forest dirt and loam, had been uncovered. Forts had been built along the way. The dragons, mandrakes, and werewolves had either been cleaned out or chased into the remote ends of the valley.

On the border where Dyonisa ended and the holy ground of the Wiyr began, an army had set up camp.

For the first time since he had started training, he saw Chuckswilly. He wore the slashlark emblem of a colonel-general and the colors of the commanding general's staff.

Jack saluted. Chuckswilly smiled and told him to be at ease.

'You're a corporal now, heh? Congratulations. Not that I didn't know about it. I've kept an eye on you. Now, tell me truly. Are you thinking about deserting to Dyonisa?'

'No, sir.'

'And why not?'

'There are many reasons, sir. You know most of them. But there's one you may not. I met a man who had been spying in Slashlark. He said that my mother and sisters and brothers had all been sent to the mines. My father left the cadmus to return to his own people. He was tried, convicted, and sentenced to the stake. But he made them kill him; he broke loose and killed two of his jailers before he died.'

Chuckswilly was silent for a moment. 'I'm grieved. I really am. I don't want to give you any false hopes, but I'll issue orders to have your family traced. Tomorrow, when we attack from here, several other places will be invaded. The mines are near one of them. I'll see to it that your family is taken care of.'

Jack's voice was thick.

'Thank you, sir.'

'I took a liking to you when I first met you, although you may not have suspected it. How would you like to be my orderly? If you do well, there'll be a sergeancy in it for you. And you won't have to be shooting at your fellow Dyonisans, unless we get in a tight spot.'

'Thank you, sir. I'd like that. However, there are some Dyonisans I wouldn't mind seeing down the barrel of my gun.'

'I know, but we can't afford bitterness, my boy. The Dyonisans left alive will be potential Socinians, we hope.'

Jack said, 'You've risen high since I last saw you, sir. Weren't you only a captain then?'

Chuckswilly smiled strangely, and he colored a little.

'It's obvious you haven't heard about my marriage. I took that beautiful witch – maybe I should say bitch – to wife. Polly is very ambitious and aggressive, as you know. She contrived, by means I'd rather not inquire into, to bring me to the notice of the marshal of our armies. Old Ananias Croatan has always had an eye, among other things, for beautiful young women. I advanced rather rapidly but not to my surprise. I feel that I am very capable.'

Jack felt his face flushing. Chuckswilly laughed and slapped him on his shoulder. 'Don't be so embarrassed, son! I knew what I was doing when I married her.'

At dawn, the army began to roll. Small compared to the forces it would soon face, it was well armored, swift, almost self-sufficient, and had tremendous firepower. It had a detailed and carefully considered plan of campaign. It had made no attempt to conceal itself, indeed, had tried to advertise. Now its 20,000 men, of whom only 8,000 were front-line fighters, faced at least 50,000. The soldiers of the Queen of Dyonisa had had plenty of time to marshal before the town of Slashlark.

It took an hour to reach the Cage farm. Jack, standing in the open turret on top of the steamer, gazed stonily at the devastation. The horns of the cadmi were blackened with fire and tilted at various angles. Craters were huge wounds in the sides of the meadow. They were the witnesses of the mines planted in holes dug beneath the cadmi and then exploded. Skeletons stuck out here and there from the snow.

Beyond, the house in which he had been born and lived all his life was a heap beneath the snow with some charred timbers sticking from the white. The barns were snowy hillocks; an overturned wagon, wheels missing, lay on its side.

Jack shut his eyes and did not open them for a long time. He could not shut out the thought that cried at him. Where was R'li? What had happened to her?

At noon, the main battle began. The armored cars and half-tracks drove forward and mowed down those facing them. A half hour later, the Socinian fleet sailed into the harbor of Slashlark and began a bombardment. Thirty dirigibles, propelled by the new oil-burning motors, dropped huge bombs.

Two hours later, the remnants of the Dyonisans had fled, and the town was taken. A mop-up force was left behind, while the rest of the army rolled on. When it came to barricades across the road, it went around. The over-all plan was to break through any sizable military organization that dared to stand up to them and to continue onward. They were travelling as swiftly as possible, their goal, the capital city. It did not matter that the countryside was alive with enemy soldiers and civilians or that they left no lines of communications or supply behind them. Before they would run out of food and ammunition, the dirigibles would drop more. And another fleet of armored steamers and wagons of infantry would follow in a few days to create more slaughter and to seize and hold some of the larger towns.

Jack had heard of the sieges of the cadmi by the Dyonisans and of the retaliatory guerrilla warfare of the horstels. Farmhouses burned to the ground were on every side. There were many cadmi that had died when the humans had dug holes under the hard shells and set off gigantic charges of powder. The horstels had fought hard, even bringing in dragons to aid them. Before the dragons had finally been killed to the last one, they had taken a high toll. And many cadmi still held out.

Now Jack rode in an enclosure, almost as big as a small house, on the back of a huge steamer. He sat at the table and received and dispatched messages over the far-speaker, the device that enabled him to talk to men as far as two thousand miles away. Occasionally he accompanied Chuckswilly to the front of the battle. Once, he had to engage in hand-to-hand fighting.

The 'punch', as the force was unofficially called, had run low on ammunition. A storm had kept the dirigibles from approaching above the town occupied by the force and dropping supplies. An unexpectedly large number of Dyonisans had charged and forced the Socinians to expend their bullets. Finally the Dyonisans broke through.

But the wind and clouds had cleared away, and the dirigables had been able to parachute in the needed ammunition. Within an hour, the new Dyonisan army was broken. Next day, the 'punch' steamed on down the highway. Thereafter, until after it had reached the city of Whittorn, it encountered little resistance. Apparently the Dyonisans were calling in all of their armies to defend the last remaining large city untaken. This was the seaport of Merrimoth, the capital after the city of Dyonis had burned down.

At Whittorn, Jack's force rendezvoused with three other task forces that had invaded Dyonisa at widely separated points along the borders. The assembled army waited for five days while supplies were brought in by dirigibles and also by heavily armored caravans. The latter had followed the same route as Jack's punch, after deciding that not enough resistance could be mustered by the enemy to stop them.

Two weeks later, Merrimoth was taken. Under the combined attack of the Socinian navy, air force, and ground forces, it crumbled. But it did not surrender. The Dyonisan soldiers fought bravely almost to a man. When their powder and bullets were spent, they used bows and arrows and spears.

Afterward, Jack stood on a hill with Chuckswilly and some high officers and watched the captured Queen being driven off to a tent reserved for her in the middle of the camp. Elizabeth III was a large but well-built woman of thirty-five with flaming red hair, straggled now, and with dirt on her aristocratic and aquiline face. She was pale but haughty, stiff-backed and resolute.

'We'll talk her into ordering her subjects to surrender,' Chuckswilly said. 'When enough of our men have followed to hold down key garrisons, we can move on to the other nations.'

Jack had automatically removed his helmet as the Queen passed him; he had been taught from childhood to do so even when her name was mentioned at public meetings. He put it back on and resumed his inspection of the burning city. The day was fair. The sun shone brightly, and it was warm for winter. The wind blew gently but steadily and carried the smoke eastward in a great layer blanketing the land and the sky above. But he was northwestward and could see everything from the height of the very high hill.

He was wondering when he would be able to find out about the fate of his mother and his brothers and sisters. Now would be a good time to approach Chuckswilly on the subject. Before, it had been impossible to make an attempt, for they had been too occupied.

He took several steps toward his commander, then stopped. He gasped.

Chuckswilly, hearing him, said, 'What's the matter? You're as white as . . . '

He gasped, too, a long, indrawn, shuddering breath. He paled under his heavy pigment. His helmet flew through the air. He cursed until he sobbed, and the tears ran down his cheeks. 'Too late! Too late! Fifty years too late!'

An object had appeared out of the blue above. It glittered and grew larger as it descended. Presently it stopped to hover a hundred feet above the burning city. A globe of some shining stuff, it must have had a diameter of at least two hundred feet. Shouts arose from the camp below the hill. Men appearing to be the size of ants swarmed about the camp grounds. Some vehicles raced off as if to escape.

Chuckswilly groaned and said, 'God! Complete victory in our grasp! And now this! On the day of our greatest triumph!'

'What do you think the Arra will do?' Jack said.

'Whatever they wish! We can't stand up to them!'

Jack felt panic rising in him. He had seen too many statues and portraits of them, heard too many tales. He said, 'Hadn't we better get out of here, sir? We can go to the Thrruk.'

Chuckswilly became calmer. 'No, we don't have to run yet. They won't start enslaving us yet, and I doubt they'll land on this hill to pick up specimens.'

There was some hope in his voice. 'Perhaps this is just a scouting expedition. If they return to their home planet to report on us, they might be gone fifty years. Maybe a hundred! Hell! There's a chance for us yet! Maybe we can make it! By God, if they do wait too long, we'll be ready for them!'

The ship slid forward, its great bulk moving swiftly and without any noise, until it came to a treeless plain on the other side of the hill. Swiftly it settled onto the plain, and the gigantic sphere sank several feet into the frozen ground.

Minutes passed. Jack and Chuckswilly and the others were silent as they waited. Presently a section of the globe swung out and one end rested on the ground. Jack sucked in a breath of fear; he was aware that his knees were shaking. When those monstrous four-footed beings shambled out onto the ramp, what would they do? Just look around and then return to the vessel or seize the nearest human beings?

Out of the darkness of the entrance of the sphere a being walked. It was a man.

'They're not Arra!' Chuckswilly said. 'Not unless they have sent some slaves out to reassure us! And they're not Egzwi either. They're not big enough!'

Then several Socinians who had been hiding in a gully at the edge of the plain slowly approached the aliens. Chuckswilly said, 'Get in the steamer, Jack. We're going down there.'

Numbly Jack obeyed. He drove the vehicle down the winding road to the bottom of the hill, then cut straight across the plain to the sphere. He halted the steamer a few yards from the opening in the ship and followed Chuckswilly. The aliens were men, no doubt of that. Most were white-skinned and had features like any Dyonisan except for a man with black skin and woolly hair and two men with eyes that had a curious fold in the corners. They all wore garments that seemed to be of one piece. These were of various colors and had emblems on them. Each man carried a small machine in one hand. Though unfamiliar-looking, they were undoubtedly weapons.

Their chief was talking, or rather, trying to talk to a sergeant of the Socinians. Chuckswilly took over and attempted to communicate but with no more success.

The chief turned to a man who must have been a linguist. This fellow tried several sentences in obviously different tongues. The black man and one of the slant-eyed men spoke.

Then Jack saw the crucifix hanging from the neck of one of the men, a crucifix half hidden in the opening of the clothing at his chest. Jack did not believe that the cross could be anything but a coincidence, for the symbol was so simple and so obvious that it must be universal. But he spoke the opening phrase of the Pater Nostrum, and several of the aliens started. The man wearing the crucifix recovered first. He rattled at Jack in Latin, completing the prayer. Afterward, he continued in Latin, although it was pronounced somewhat differently than the Dyonisan priests spoke it. Jack looked helpless, for he knew very little Latin beyond that spoken in the Mass.

He explained to Chuckswilly, who sent a soldier off posthaste to find a priest. Within an hour, the soldier returned with a very scared priest, Bishop Passos, who had been captured with the Queen. But the bishop recovered swiftly enough when he began to understand the alien with the crucifix. Thereafter the bishop became attached, willy nilly, as Chuckswilly's official interpreter.

Bishop Passos said, 'They come from Earth! Glory to God, they are Earthmen! And he' – indicating the speaker of Latin – 'is a priest of the Holy Roman Catholic Church; he has spoken to the Pope on Earth!'

Chuckswilly, as always, was quick to adapt. In an aside to Jack, he said, 'I wonder if he'll be so joyous when he finds out that the Earth priest will regard him as a heretic. He has no idea of how greatly Dyonisan Catholicism has deviated from the original religion. Or, if he does, he's forgotten.'

The bishop then said, 'Father Goodrich says we must be mistaken. *We* don't speak English! *They* do!'

'Two different brands,' Chuckswilly said. 'The languages have deviated. Ask them if they would like to visit our general. Or, if they don't trust us, and I don't blame them, if we could see their ship.'

Via the two interpreters, the captain of the Earthmen replied that he would visit their general in his tent. This fearlessness indicated that the Earthmen felt secure; Jack guessed that they must have very powerful weapons. He lost his joy and began wondering if they might be as much a menace as the Arra. Looking at Chuckswilly's expression, he knew that his commander was thinking the same.

In the tent of General Florz, the Darians and the Terrestrials talked until late at night. Jack was allowed to attend Chuckswilly, so he heard every word of the conversation. When the Earthmen discovered that the Darians were descendants of the lost colony of Roanoke and others who had been abducted, it was their turn to be amazed. But the news of the Arra and the Egzwi alarmed them. They questioned the bishop in detail. Jack, knowing that they used a variety of English, listened carefully. After a half hour, he was able to understand a few words.

In turn, Chuckswilly and the general questioned the aliens. How had they managed to cross space? What kind of power did they use? What was Earth like?

The aliens seemed to reply frankly. Many of their answers were disquieting. Jack wondered if the whole planet had gone crazy. Could sane human beings really live like that and remain sane? Yet they claimed to be happy and prosperous.

Through the interpreters, Captain Swanson of the interstellar vessel *United* explained that his craft was the first to land on an inhabited planet – as far as he knew. Two other survey vessels were to leave Earth, shortly after his departure, for different destinations. The personnel of the *United* had gone into deep freeze for the thirty Earth years it had taken for the vessel to arrive in the neighborhood of Dare's sun. After automatic equipment had thawed them out, they had examined the likely planets for life. For some days, they had been circling this planet. Looking through instruments capable of very powerful magnification, they had been astonished to find beings that exactly resembled their own species, a highly improbable event. They had also seen the horstels in detail and knew that they were of a different species or subspecies.

Chuckswilly told them that horstels had also been brought to this planet by the Arra.

Captain Swanson replied that the report of the Arra and the Egzwi disturbed him very much. They represented a possible danger to Earth.

Chuckswilly said, 'To take word of them to Earth, you would have to go back in the ship, wouldn't you? Or do you have a means of communicating across space?'

Swanson smiled. He must have guessed that Chuckswilly had another reason besides the surface reason for asking. But he answered frankly. They had means of communicating, but they couldn't wait sixty years for an answer from Earth.

Chuckswilly said, 'You'll be wanting to inform Earth as soon as possible of the Arra. After all, the Arra have been to Earth at least twice that we know of. The next time, they might come to conquer. And the next time might be soon. Too soon.'

Swanson replied, 'You're a very shrewd man. I won't lie to you. We are alarmed. Originally, we'd intended to stay here several years before leaving. Now we have no choice but to take off in a very short time.'

'I would like to know, I must know,' Chuckswilly said, 'if you Earthmen consider the planet of Dare to be your property?'

Swanson was silent for a moment before speaking.

'No,' he said slowly. 'The government formulated a hands-off policy for any planet that might be inhabited. Planets that are unpopulated by sentients but are livable are to be claimed in the name of Earth, provided there's no prior claim by extraterrestrials.

'No, we make no claims. But we would like to make a treaty establishing our right to build a base here. After all, that would be to your benefit even more than to ours. In your present state of technology, you need Earth's help. And the next ship will undoubtedly contain many scientists whose knowledge will further yours.'

'I doubt,' Chuckswilly said drily, 'that we could do much to stop you – if we so felt inclined.'

'We're not to use force,' Swanson replied.

'But the news of the Arra might change your government's mind,' Chuckswilly said.

Swanson shrugged and said that he wished to return to the *United*. His face was impassive, but there was something about him that suggested that he would not be surprised by a refusal by the Socinians. Chuckswilly and the general, however, were certain that Swanson would not have accepted their invitation if he had thought they could enforce any aggression. Moreover, they suspected that all that had been said had been monitored by those in the ship.

After the aliens had left, Chuckswilly spoke to Jack. 'I don't like this. When they return and build a base – all for our protection, of course – we'll inevitably be dominated. Their culture is too superior. Dare will become the Earth's appendage; Darian ways will become Earth ways.'

'We'll have at least sixty years to catch up,' Jack said.

'Don't be dense! They will have progressed by sixty years, too. And we lack the mineral resources of Earth.'

'Some Darians ought to go back with them,' Jack said. 'Then they could learn about Earth and its knowledge. They might be able to help us enormously when they returned.'

'By the Great Dragon, boy! You may have something there.'

They returned to the tent. Jack heated some totum water, and he sat down to drink with his superior. In private, Chuckswilly was very democratic.

'We're in a pickle, Jack. We can't get along without Earth's help. But if we accept it, we lose as Darians.'

He struck his fist on the tabletop. 'Damn! Just on the verge of triumph, too!'

'You've told me more than once that I should accept the "inevitable course of history,"' Jack said. 'You were talking about Socinia's course then, which seemed destined to conquer. Now history is on the side of the Earthmen. Why can't *you* accept the "inevitable destiny"?'

Chuckswilly glared. But in a few seconds his brow cleared, and he laughed. 'Hoist with his own petard! Well, not necessarily.'

He was silent for a while. Jack refilled their cups. Chuckswilly said, 'If we could seize the crew and then the ship, the knowledge we'd gain thereby would give our science an enormous impetus. It's possible that, by the time another Earth ship came along, we might be able to meet them on more than equal terms.'

He stood up. 'General Florz said he was too tired to talk tonight, that we'd discuss this tomorrow. No, by the Dragon! We'll talk about it tonight! This is not a time for sleep!'

He told Jack he did not need him, and he left. Jack sat for a while, thinking, began yawning, and got ready for bed. It seemed to him that he had just closed his eyes when he was being shaken awake.

A sergeant was standing over him.

Jack blinked in the pale light of the oil lantern hanging from the cord in the middle of the tent. He said, 'What in hell's wrong, Sergeant?'

'You must be a great lover, you dog,' the sergeant said. 'There's a woman outside the camp. She says that she has to see you; that it'd be all right to wake you up. Now, when in hell did you get time to even talk to a woman?'

Jack sat up and began to put on his boots. 'I haven't.'

He stood up, very excited. 'Maybe it's my mother or one of my sisters. Oh, God, maybe they got out of the mines alive!'

'She's too young to be your mother. Must be your sister.'

'Didn't she say who she was?'

'No. Just said she was one of the women on your father's farm.'

'Lunk's daughter?' Jack said. 'Was she dark and bony-faced?'

'No, she was blonde and good-looking.'

'Elizabeth!'

Jack ran out of the tent, then returned when the sergeant reminded him that he had left his revolver and rifle behind. It was death for a soldier to be caught unarmed during the campaign.

Jack thanked him and resumed his running. Near the borders of the camp, he slowed to a fast walk. He did not want some triggerskitty sentry shooting at him.

The camp had been ringed by the steamers, all of which pointed outward. Every third one had at least two men standing duty by it, and these had built fires outside to keep warm. A sentry challenged him; Jack gave the proper password. He asked the fellow where the woman who wanted Jack Cage was. The sentry pointed at a small fire about a hundred and fifty yards outside the camp. That was as close as the woman had been allowed to come.

He ran across the frozen ground, his breath coming out in steam. During the day, the snow was thawing, but it was still quite cold at night. He almost slipped on a thin patch of snow. Then he was with the heavily bundled figure that had been standing by the fire.

'Elizabeth!' he cried. He enfolded her in his arms and began to weep.

A soft familiar voice murmured, 'No, Jack. R'li.'

He stepped back. For a moment, he could not speak.

'You? What . . . how? What are you doing here? I thought . . . ?'

'I went back to my home, Jack. But the cadmi had already been blown up. Everybody was dead. So, I went to the valley in the Thrruk. But we heard about the war between the humans and the Wiyr. We could not stay there in safety while our fellows were being slaughtered. We organized in small harrying groups; I was in one.

'Finally, after almost being killed or captured several times, I was forced into taking refuge in a cadmus that was still holding out. We thought we would all be dead in a few days, because the humans had dug great holes under the cadmi boneplates and were getting ready to place mines under it.

'Then we heard about the Socinians. Our besiegers left us; I suppose they joined in defense of Merrimoth. I hoped that you would be in the invading Socinian force, so I came here. And . . . here I am.'

Jack crushed her to him and kissed her violently. 'You don't know how I missed you!' he said over and over.

'I was afraid that you would hate me because I left you.'

'I did for a long time. Finally I told myself that you could not help yourself. You had been a horstel too long. Then I began missing you. There were nights when I couldn't sleep because of thinking about you. I planned to go looking for you when this was over. But I never really expected to find you. It would have been too good of God to have permitted me to love you again, to hold you in my arms.'

He stood irresolute. 'I can't let you stay out here all alone. There are too many stragglers around. I don't want to find you just to lose you. But I can't take you back to camp with me. They're strict as hell about discipline.

'Still, the Earthmen – you've heard about them, yes? – have made a change in our plans. We'll stay here until something is settled. So . . . but where can you be safe?'

'My cadmus is only five miles away. Even though it's so close to Merrimoth, it's a large one and situated on top of a plateau on a high hill. It was easily defended; the humans lost many before they forced us to go underground. I can return there and be safe.'

'I'll go back with you as far as your home,' he said. 'I don't want you killed by any skulkers. Hell, I'll desert! I'll stay with you!'

She smiled, shook her head, and touched him lovingly. 'No, I won't allow you to place yourself in peril again for me. If the Socinians came after you, they'd shoot you. No.'

'I'll at least go back with you.'

'It's not necessary. I have an escort hiding back in the shadows. I am the daughter of an O-Reg, you know.'

They talked for an hour, kissed, wished they could have some privacy. Then, gently but firmly, R'li said *au revoir*, and she walked away into the darkness. Jack returned to camp, where he had to endure some obscene but good-natured jests. By the time he got back to the tent, it was dawn. Chuckswilly met him outside the flap.

Surprised, he asked Jack Cage where he had been. Jack told him. Chuckswilly seemed pleased, but his spirits soon faded. He had Jack make some more hot totum water.

'Florz was too stunned and awed to take any action. I didn't think he was going to do anything. We can't just sit here on our numb butts, so I farspoke to headquarters in Socinia. They agreed they need a man who can take positive action. They spoke to Florz. He was no longer much use to them. So, tomorrow, he returns to Socinia to get a hero's welcome. Big parade, speeches, flowers, wine, women.

'I'm now in command.'

Chuckswilly rose from the table, clenched his hands behind him, and paced back and forth.

'It's not been an easy decision to make. If we attack, we will probably be annihilated. Or the ship will just rise into the air and leave us helpless. If we do nothing, we may get a few crumbs of knowledge from their lordly table. But not much. They wouldn't want us to know too much. We might be too well armed when they return.

'We need their science. The Arra might come before the Earthmen's second ship does. We'd be helpless. Furthermore, if we could seize the ship and its crew, it might be a hundred years or more before another Earth ship came this way. And when it did, we'd be ready for them and for the Arra and the Egzwi, also.'

'You intend to attack, sir?'

'Yes. But how! As long as the ship is sealed shut, we could do nothing. Our cannons wouldn't hurt it, I'll bet my kilt on that. Nor can we get close enough to rush inside when the port opens. Their captain was kind enough to let me know that they have detection devices that would forestall that.

'In fact, for all I know, my words may even now be overheard by their devilish machines!'

'It seems to me, sir, that you have only two chances and those not very good. You can seize the captain and whoever is with him when they next come out. Or you can talk him into taking some Socinians back to Earth with him. Then, somehow, the Socinians seize the ship and return with it.'

'Socinian passengers wouldn't be able to steer that vessel. Even if they should force some Earthmen to do it for them, it's likely that the Earthmen would wreck the vessel rather than allow it to fall in our hands. There's always a hero or two aboard any ship.

'But . . . hmmm! . . . if enough of us could get invited aboard for dinner or an inspection trip, then . . . '

'They'd take precautions against treachery.'

'It wouldn't be treachery if we didn't give our word not to attempt anything.'

Chuckswilly abruptly went to bed and Jack did the same a few minutes later. However, he had slept only two hours when his superior awakened him. The Earth vessel had opened its port ramp again, and Swanson and others had come out. This time they were in a vehicle of their own. It was small, needle-shaped, and floated several feet off the ground. It was heading toward the camp.

Chuckswilly flew into a frenzy of action. He gave instructions to twelve officers, made them repeat them, so there would be no mistake. If they saw him give a certain signal, they would jump upon the men, as planned, and overpower them. The aliens were to be silenced at once, and the officers were also to be silenced. Should the Earthmen have devices on them that could transmit sound to the ship, the devices must register nothing suspicious. Captain Swanson would then be taken away out of earshot of the others, stripped of any far-speaking equipment, and told what he must do if he wished to live. If he agreed, then he must be returned at once to the group so that he could talk as if nothing had happened. Meanwhile, the others would be removed and given the same choice as the captain. Then the aliens and their captors would go to the ship. They would enter, and the Socinians would attempt to hold the port open long enough for a force, which was already stationed at the edge of the plain, to rush in.

To effect Chuckswilly's plan, the Socinians would take the Earthmen's hand-weapons, find out how to fire them, and then use them inside the ship.

If Chuckswilly's men observed no signal during the conference, they should treat the Earthmen as honored guests.

'It's a weak and wild plan,' Chuckswilly said to Jack. 'A weakness and wildness born out of desperation. If one of Swanson's officers decides to sacrifice himself to save the ship and yells, we've lost. Even if we get inside the ship, we may not be able to get to the control room – whatever a control room looks like!'

The Earthmen arrived. They were surprised to find that Chuckswilly was now general, but they complimented him. Swanson said that he had decided that the Arra were too important to Earth to delay reporting about them. The *United* would leave within a week.

However, he did want to make arrangements to leave a certain number of technicians, engineers, and scientists behind. These would not only gather data on the planet and its life and history but would help actively in Socinia's progress. Convinced that the Socinians would not only win their campaigns but should, because Dare would then be a single people, the Earthmen had decided to recognize Socinia as the *de facto* government of the planet.

'However,' Swanson continued, through the two interpreters, 'it's necessary that we make an official treaty. It's equally important that we establish a base for those we're leaving behind. We will leave certain equipment there, and our men will operate out of there. I suggest that some of your men, perhaps even you, General Chuckswilly, come with us to Socinia's captal. You can explain to the head of your state who and what we are and what we'd like.'

Chuckswilly smiled. Only Jack knew what lay behind that smile. Chuckswilly said, 'Our army should continue at once to the borders. But you are even more important than the conquest. My colonel-general can lead our forces while I accompany you to Greathopes.'

'Would you like to complete your conquests with an absolute minimum of bloodshed?' Swanson said. 'If you could hold up your advances, we might be able to supply you later with the means.'

Chuckswilly said that that was more than generous. What was this means?

'We have several that could do the job,' the alien captain replied. 'But I was specifically thinking of a gas which would render your enemy unconscious for a few hours. We also have a device for paralyzing individual combatants at short range, out of gunshot, that is.'

'Very well,' Chuckswilly said briskly. 'I'll make all the arrangements with the capital by farspeaker. And I'll take about ten of my staff with me.'

'I'm sorry, but we don't have accommodations for that many,' Swanson said.

Chuckswilly hid his frustration and the knowledge that the captain was lying. He asked if he could take at least four, and Swanson agreed. They left without Chuckswilly giving the signal.

Jack said, 'May I take R'li along, sir? I'd like to see her safe in Socinia.'

'Not a bad idea. Maybe if the Earthmen see us bring a female along, they'll worry less about our trying to seize the ship.'

'You're still thinking about doing that?'

'If I get the slightest chance,' Chuckswilly said. He wrote some names on a paper and handed the paper to Jack. 'Now, before you go for your siren, summon these men. They're bold and quick.'

Several hours later Jack drove back into the camp with R'li beside him. He had explained to her what might happen and told her that it might be better if she did not come with him. But she had insisted that she preferred to be with him.

On the way back to camp, Jack had said, 'I've been thinking about what Swanson said. That Earthmen are one now, Earthmen everywhere. But the Socinians don't want that. They want Dare for themselves. Yet they argue that their war is justified because it will unite Dare and make it strong enough to present a solid front against the Arra or Egzwi.

'Now the tables are turned. Earth could make us one. And we need them, they're an absolute necessity. So what if we do lose our language, our religions, our customs? They are lost just as much under Socinian rule. Besides, they don't matter. Chuckswilly himself said that they would have to perish; a new culture will arise. The difference now is that it'll be Earth culture, not Socinian.'

'What do you intend to do about it?' she said.

'I don't know, I was a traitor to my country once because I believed that it was an evil thing. Can I be a traitor a second time? I'd be even more justified in this situation. But I'm in agony. Was I a traitor because I have no loyalty and I'm an opportunist? Or are my motives really justified?'

On arriving at the general's tent, Jack and R'li were greeted by Chuckswilly. He took Jack aside and said, 'You won't have to do anything while we're on the ship. In fact, to show the Earthmen I intend no treachery, you, R'li, the priest, and myself will be the only ones going.'

'Why?' Jack said. He knew Chuckswilly well enough to guess that he had a far better plan.

'There's a meadow near the People's House,' Chuckswilly said, referring to the mansion in which the Socinian head of state lived. 'Thousands of men are digging like barefoxes now. They'll plant a huge quantity of mines in the hole, cover it up, and replace the grass. I'll direct the Earthmen to land there. There's no reason why they should refuse, they're so smug about their invulnerability. After the port has been opened for the Earth delegation and us to go to the People's House, the mines will be set off.

'We don't think the explosion will harm the ship in the slightest. But the shock waves going through the vessel should either kill the occupants or knock them out. Our soldiers will rush in immediately after the explosion, board, and take the ship.'

Chuckswilly walked back and forth, grinning triumphantly.

'What about the next Earth expedition?' Jack said.

'If we're ready, we fight them. If not, we won't even have to let them know that the *United* ever came to Dare. And we'll take them too!'

Chuckswilly continued talking and did not stop until word came that Swanson was ready to go. Chuckswilly said he was not quite ready yet. He got into contact with the capital via farspeaker to inquire how far the work on the mine-trap had progressed. He was told to delay for another two hours. Chuckswilly sent a message to Swanson that the Socinian president was still in conference with his cabinet on terms of the treaty. But he would send word as soon as the conference was ended. The Earthmen did not need to be in any hurry, since they had said the ship could fly to the capital in an hour.

'That'll give us at least three hours,' Chuckswilly said to Jack.

Jack thought the time would never arrive. He sat by the farspeaker, waiting for a message from the capital. R'li sat on a chair near him. She looked strange to him in clothes; moreover, she had a strained expression. Finally, when Chuckswilly had left the tent for a minute, Jack said, 'What are you thinking?'

'At first, I was thinking about the old ways and how they're lost forever. You can't possibly know what this means to a Wiyr. Despite the faults of human society, humans are more adaptable – as a general rule. However, I can make the change. To survive, I must.

'But Socinia, which once represented the new ways, has suddenly become the old itself. Its ideals, if ever they were valid, are no longer so. Therefore, it should go down into the dust as surely as the humans and horstels went down before the horman. It's logical and just.'

Jack did not reply, but he was thinking much. Two hours passed. An additional half hour. Then the farspeaker came to life. The trap was set.

Chuckswilly, Jack, R'li, and Bishop Passos rode out to the *United*. They carried no weapons, for Chuckswilly wanted to convince the Earthmen that no treachery was intended. They entered; the port closed; the vessel left the ground.

Captain Swanson and Father Goodrich wore small black boxes, suspended by cords from their necks. From each box, a wire ran to a plug inserted in the wearer's ear. Swanson took similar boxes from a table and handed one to each Darian. Through the priests, he explained.

'This device should help us to speak without too much recourse to interpreters. My converter will receive your English speech, give those words that need it the vowel values of my English, and transmit the words as speech with Terrestrial English pronunciation – General Midwestern American, to be specific.

'It's not a perfect interpreter, because your English has quite a few vocabulary differences. You've retained words that have dropped out of our speech. Some that both speeches still use now have different meanings. You've borrowed a number of words from the horstels. And your syntax is somewhat different. However, I think we can manage at least a ninety-per-cent understanding.

'Your devices convert my vowel pronunciations into yours.'

They tried out the converters. Although the words coming

into his ear sounded metallic and inhuman, and the vowel correspondences were not quite exact, Jack soon got over his uncomfortable feeling. He could comprehend most of what Swanson said. The main difficulty was that he could hear Swanson speaking with double voices. However, since Swanson's native speech was unintelligible, it was only a distracting noise. Jack learned to ignore it.

The captain guided them on a tour of inspection of the vessel. Jack and R'li and the bishop made no effort to hide their astonishment and awe. Chuckswilly gave forth with a few ah's, but most of the time his face was stony.

After the tour, Swanson told them that dinner was to be served. Would they like to wash before eating? His manner made it clear that he would be both surprised and offended if they did not. The bishop went into one washroom; Chuckswilly, into the other. Jack and R'li waited their turn. Chuckswilly had hesitated for several seconds before leaving, and Jack knew that he did not want to leave him alone with the Earthmen. But protocol demanded that Chuckswilly, as Jack's superior, use the washroom first.

It was then that Jack made up his mind. It was now or never, for he doubted that he would again be left alone with Swanson. Moreover, in thirty minutes, the ship would land at Greathopes.

He said, 'Captain, I have something to tell you.'

Several minutes later, the bishop and the general came out of the washrooms. Jack entered the one previously used by his superior, and he took his time cleaning up. When he came out, reluctantly, he found a pale and silent group. R'li, however, smiled at him.

Chuckswilly glared and said, 'Traitor!'

Jack was trembling with a guilt that he had told himself he had no reason to feel. But he succeeded in making his voice firm.

'I decided to tell Swanson for exactly the same reasons that I decided to join the Socinians. You were the one who convinced me in both cases.'

'We may as well go eat – if anybody has any appetie left,' Swanson said.

Chuckswilly swallowed hard. 'I bow to the inevitable course of destiny. It is more important, I suppose, that mankind survive as a united species than as separate and warring nationalities. But it's hard to give up dreams.'

'Those who've opposed you in the past and lost must have found it just as difficult to give up their dreams,' Swanson said.

Twenty minutes later the city of Greathopes appeared. It sprawled out in a valley surrounded by towering sharp-peaked mountains. The *United* flew straight for the landing field prepared for it. However, it halted several thousand feet above and to one side of the field. Five minutes passed. Suddenly the ground below was hidden. Smoke billowed up to form a giant mushroom-shaped cloud.

Swanson said to Chuckswilly, 'If I wished, I could order the entire city to be scanned by our explosive-activating beams. Every bit of gunpowder in the area would be set off. If I were so inclined, I could do the same with every foot of land on this continent.'

The ship settled down toward the edge of the broad deep hole that had been a smooth meadow.

Three days later the treaty was concluded. In a week the Earthmen's base was built in almost magical speed and with incredible means. And the *United* left Dare.

Jack and R'li stayed the winter in the Earthmen's base. Both were teachers of their respective languages. The linguists who recorded them explained that they were not interested so much in being able to speak them as they were in preserving them for scientific study. They expected that Socinian, the pidgin fusion of English and horstel, would absorb both speeches.

Chuckswilly, hearing this, had snorted and said, 'What they're not about to say is that they also expect Terrestrial English to kill off Socinian. But that's at some distant date.'

Chuckswilly had given an official promise to Swanson that no reprisals would be taken against Cage for having disclosed the attempt to seize the *United*. Jack and R'li were not sure that he could be trusted to keep his word. But the only alternative was to go on the ship to Earth, and they did not want that. Better to take their chances in a world they knew, although changing, than in an absolutely new, complex, bewildering, and alien society.

Spring came. One sunny morning, Jack and R'li were transported in one of the flying machines that the *United* had left behind to the site of the Cage farm. The Earthmen deposited several tents, food, weapons, and tools. They wished the two good luck and took off.

Jack watched the needle of the boat until it was merged with the blue of the sky. R'li, big with child, stood by him. Afterward, he forced himself to look at the desolation revealed by the thawing snow. It would take several years before he could build a house and barn large and strong enough to satisfy him. There, where the ruins of his father's house lay, he would build a small cabin out of logs. Later, when a few crops had come in, and more babies were born, he would add more rooms.

Plowing would have been a great task, for he had no unicorns and not much prospect of getting any. But the Terrestrials had promised to bring him a steamer plow later. He hoped they would not forget. Although he knew they were now thankful because he had saved their lives, he also knew that gratitude could be short-lived.

R'li kissed him on his cheek. 'Don't worry.'

'At least, I'll be doing what I know and love. I was getting tired of being cooped up in the base building and teaching a language doomed to die. But everything now is so uncertain and dangerous. My own people are going to be hostile. And it'll be some time before the Socinian occupation forces will be able to stamp out underground rebels and the mountain raiders. Moreover, Chuckswilly may be waiting for a chance to get revenge. He could have us killed and blame it on Dyonisan rebels.'

She took his hand, and she said, 'You're in no more peril than when all this started. Life is always uncertain; death is around every corner. Let us build our houses, till our soil, and raise children. We will hate no one and hope that no one hates us, knowing full well that there is as much hate as love in this world.

'Whatever happens then, we will be doing our best for ourselves, our children, and our neighbors. That is the least we can do, not the most. It won't be easy. The only easy thing is to give up.'